# DEMONS
# AMONG US

## W. E.
## ZAZO-PHILLIPS

*Demons Among Us* is a work of fiction. Any names, characters, places, and incidents utilized or described are the products of the author's imagination or are used fictitiously. Any resemblance to actual events, locales, or persons, living or dead, is entirely coincidental.

1

The author would like to thank:

all of the outstanding Coastguardsmen and Sea Daddies I have encountered throughout my military career, including: BMC Timothy Molly, ASTCS Richard Bielewicz, CWO Chris Johnson; MKC Burl Boone; CWO Ray Colicci; EMC Barry King; DCC Jason Kotz; HSMC Ron Hill and his wife, Paula; DCC Joe Longstreet; EMC Brian Rader; YNC Shellie Chambers; Conrad "Red" Wilkie; and CWO Brent Nasworthy and his wife, Ginny.

Special thanks to CWO Peter Wolf, who did me the great favor of talking me out of an angry farewell gesture involving       tampons, corn syrup, ketchup, and the engineers' boondockers; I wouldn't have made it off the cutter alive.

Fair winds and following seas to you all.

my readers, Ben Schrecengost and Ray Fishburne, for the boost of confidence.

the Examiners of Selection Services, whose guidance and feedback have greatly improved my understanding of the writing process.

Travis Leichssenring of K Studio (http://web.mac.com/kharum), for his support and vision.

Marc Grossman, his wife Gemma, and the monthly Traveler group, whose members are infinitely patient with my lapses of attention during game play when the writing gets the best of me.

This book is dedicated to my husband and my children: you make my life worthwhile.

2

# ◆ PROLOGUE ◆

*New Brunswick, New Jersey*
*Not Long Ago*

*"Fa li' ga eh waa fa meh…"*

*She could smell copper, sweet and nauseating, in the air. She was standing in a white-walled room in front of an indoor pool with brownish tiles…no… they were white tiles, too…but the water was dark and murky. Films of reds and rust browns covered the tile floor, the walls--everything. There were several people in grimy swim suits thrashing around, screaming, their faces contorted. Some of them were cut and bleeding, growing pale as they frantically pulled their bodies through the water.*

*"Cach a shee acriss da sea…"*

*Then she realized that the water was more than churning—it was boiling. Some people were scalded, their faces peeling, but others were not.*

*"Sal ha shee boot, all ala…"*

*Then her attention was focused on someone coming up to the surface. It was a woman, wearing a bathrobe, except the front was opened, showing black and charred breasts and a black flaking torso. Her hair and scalp were gone, and her skull looked like an egg…*

*"Neva knaeef I ma et ham…"*

*… in her hand she saw a flash of metal …*

*"Louie Louie…"*

Jessica English woke up with a start, sickened and biting back a scream. She always had vivid dreams, but this one was so different. She could smell the chorine and the burning flesh as she watched the carnage. The echoes of the screams were still ringing in her ears. It was as if it had just happened for real—not a dream. Jessica had never experienced anything like that before.

She drew up her knees and wrapped her arms around them, trying to calm down. Even after a few minutes, she couldn't get rid of the shakes entirely. She remembered that the woman whose scalp had melted off was attacking the others, but the woman wasn't acting like herself. Jessica paused.

*"Wasn't acting like herself?"* Where'd that come from?

How Jessica could have known that about the woman, she wasn't certain, but it was like the woman was…possessed or something?

*Well, it might be an interesting story,* she thought. It was Saturday, and she had the day off from Home Depot. She climbed out of bed and turned on her computer.

Jessica was going to school for psychology, but she hoped to also write professionally someday. Though she got ideas from life all the time, she often got her best ideas from her dreams. Once she got them written, she posted them on storyline.com, a workshop-type site where writers could publish and critique stories. She had tried to get her friends at school to read her stories, but they never seemed to have the time.

Several hours later, she was finished. It was a simple story about a possessed woman on the rampage, but it surprised Jessica how easily the plot came to her. She read it a few times. It didn't even need much polishing. She still felt a little creeped out, but writing it down made her feel a lot better. Satisfied, she sent the document through the spellchecker, logged onto storyline.com, and published it as a new short story.

Only then it occurred to her than to look at the clock. It was 2:00 pm, and she had an hour until her study group.

*Crap!* She logged off and ran to the shower.

Half a continent away, Todd Olson noticed KnightWhoSaysNEE! had a new story.

*She's usually good,* he thought, clicking on the title Beelzebub Returns.

When he got to the part about the pool, he blinked. He read it again. He blinked. He turned to his wife, Chris, who was watching TV behind him.

"Honey? Could you describe your dream again?"

Chris frowned. "OK. It was a white pool, and there were people getting cut up…"

A few minutes later, Todd wrote a private e-mail to Knight:

I guess I'll just go ahead and ask: did you get your idea from a dream? This is going to sound weird, but my wife described the climax of your story to a "T."

Milk Toddy

He got a reply a few hours later:

What's your home phone number?

Knight

"What should we do?" Jessica asked Chris over the phone a few minutes later. "Do you think anyone else has had these dreams?"

"No idea," Chris replied.

"Hey," Todd interrupted over the living room phone. "I just found a site that talks about prophesy through dream interpretation. They encourage people who have shared dreams to post. Want to?"

"Where is it?" Jessica asked, sitting down at the computer.

"Ummm…www.dreamprophesy.com."

Jessica typed it in. Swirls of colors appeared on the screen, followed by chubby angels unfurling a banner with the site name emblazoned in gold letters.

*Cute.*

She clicked on the "message board" button. There were a few posts on the forum, but nothing within the past six months. All the posts were questions about dream research. No one posted about specific dreams, but Jessica supposed not too many people shared dreams.

"Seems harmless enough," Jessica said. "Why not?" She began to type.

There was a knock at the door.

*What the fuck?* Jessica thought, turning over after trying to get to sleep. Maybe it was a drunk at the wrong door. It figures her roommate went home that weekend--she would have been up and at the door in a second.

Another knock, this one louder. "Miss English?" she heard. "Are you there?"

"Yes?" she called, throwing back the covers. "Who's there?"

"Police, ma'am." The voice replied.

She threw on a robe and went to the door. The distorted men on the other side of the keyhole were wearing blue uniforms. "Can I see some ID?"

The one in front flashed a badge.

She unbolted the door and opened it. There were two men in police uniforms standing in front of her. They were both in their mid-thirties and tall. Jessica was sure their hair was cropped short under their hats.

"What happened?" she asked the two officers. "What's wrong?"

"May we come in, Ms. English?" the one with the badge asked. "We need to speak to you."

Jessica stepped back and let the two men in. "I'm leaving the door opened. Is that OK?"

"Sure," the other cop said, looking around the room. "We prefer that." He stared for a moment at the black and white poster of Albert Einstein sticking his tongue out, and then took a breath.

"I'm Officer Smith, this is Officer Melendez. Ms. English, is your roommate Deborah Swanson?"

Jessica felt her blood run icy. "Yes--what's happened to her? Is she all right?"

Melendez stepped forward and removed his hat. His hair was cut short, and was almost totally gray.

"Ms. English, your roommate was found dead three hours ago. We're pretty sure it was foul play. She didn't die well."

Jessica felt her legs give way as she sank down onto Deborah's bed. She never really liked Debbie, but she never knew someone who was murdered before. The cop followed her down into a crouch beside her.

"Oh, my God..." Jessica began. Thoughts began to pour out...

*What did Debbie do? Who could have done it? Is it someone I know?*

"There's more." The cops exchanged glances. "There was a note with the body, suggesting you will be next."

Jessica heard herself gasp.

"You need to come with us. We will protect you, but..."

"But," Jessica protested, "We don't hang out. We don't know the same people..."

She felt herself began to panic. It wasn't fair. She leapt up from the bed, tears streaming down her face. She felt fear and terror coming in waves...

"Now, Ms. English," Melendez said, taking her hands. "We don't have time for this."

Jessica heard him, but she couldn't calm herself. She began to gulp for air.

Melendez turned and gave the other cop a pleading glance.

Smith stepped forward. A handkerchief magically appeared in his hand. He offered it to Jessica.

5

Jessica reached out and took the handkerchief. She dabbed at her eyes and wiped her nose. *Strange cologne*, Jessica thought. *Like flowers, but a little metallic.* Jessica finished drying her eyes and reached up to hand the handkerchief back Smith. She already felt a little better...

A moment later, Melendez caught Jessica as she slumped over onto Deborah's bed, unconscious. Smith quickly walked over and shut the door.

"She out?" Smith asked.

"Oh, yeah," Melendez answered, standing up. He reached into his left coat pocket and grabbed a clean handkerchief. He used it to pick up the handkerchief in Jessica's right hand and put it into a plastic baggie, also acquired from his coat pocket. When all the items were secure and back in their places, he turned to his partner.

"See anything she would want?" he asked.

Smith looked around. "Well, once she's debriefed she can come back for her own stuff. And, if she doesn't, well..." The man shrugged. "It wouldn't matter, anyway."

"Right," Melendez agreed. Pulling Jessica to her feet, he ducked his head under Jessica's arm and pulled her next to him. "Can you get the door?"

"Yup," Smith said, opening the door. "You got her?"

"Oh, yes," Melendez answers, pulling Jessica along. "She's as light as a feather. Can't be more than a buck ten, buck twenty. Don't forget the hard drive."

"Yup."

A few minutes later, the one or two students on the quad who stopped to watch saw two cops carry an obviously stoned or drunk Jessica to their patrol car. They carefully lay her down in the backseat, and then speed away. Their lights and siren remained off.

No one thought anything about it. Someone always took their partying too far on Saturday nights in the dorms...

That Sunday evening, Deborah Swanson returned to her dorm room to find a note on Jessica's bed that she was going home for a few days. Two weeks later, two men who identified themselves as Jessica's brothers came by to get her stuff.

"Yup," the blond, freckle-faced one named Joe explained, "She came home and realized she was too homesick to go back to school. Dad was pissed. 'All that money down the toilet!' he said. Mom's happy, though."

Deborah, who liked Jessica well enough but was now looking forward to having the room to herself for the rest of the semester, agreed that it was probably for the best Jessica stay at home.

After they left, though, Deborah tried to remember if Jessica had ever mentioned having brothers. She had really thought Jessica was an only child...

# ✦CHAPTER ONE✦

*50 Miles S-SE of Miami, Florida*
*Five Days before Infusion*

The engines of the *Surveyor* were at all-stop. The engine room was relatively quiet, with the exception of the ticking and purring of the generators and the hum of the oil heaters. With double hearing protection on, they only whispered. The two-hundred seventy foot Coast Guard Cutter, or "270", had gone limp when the engines died, and now she let the waves have their way with her, tossing and rolling the cutter and pitching within the troughs. The pitching and dipping made the new crewmembers puke. For those who had been on board a while, though, it felt like nothing at all.

On this particular day, a woman sat perched on top of a steel trashcan inside the helo hanger in the heart of the Caribbean Sea. Through the wide opening of the hanger she could see a sunny day, and the deep blue ocean waters stretched forever with nothing to cease their eternal reach outward. From her perspective, though, she mostly saw the dark expanse of the cave-like helo hanger with bits and pieces scattered everywhere, followed by yards and yards of grey non-skid deck with painted white circles and then, every few seconds, slivers of the Caribbean blue sea peeking over the flight deck as the cutter swayed about. The ship had set the Law Enforcement Detail the day before, and she watched the freighter under search gently bobbing 500 yards off the starboard rear quarter. Its engines, too, were shut off, but the freighter was built with smoother lines--it hardly rocked at all.

There was a third class cook standing next to the woman, smoking a cigarette, but neither one said anything. As she raised her cigar to her lips a gold wedding band glinted on her left hand. It was one of her last cigars, a nice Dominican Montecristo knockoff, but she had one more left in her locker, for the Special Sea Detail approaching Rhode Island, and her homeport, about a week from now.

There was "hot intel" that drugs were on board, but the female knew this was a waste of time. Everyone on the cutter knew by now the drugs were not behind the aft fuel tank like they were supposed to be. Most likely, the captain saw the large blinding-white 270-foot ship approaching at a mere 14 knots in the noonday sun, ate lunch, took a long shit, and then got rid of the contraband before the *Surveyor* managed to catch up and pull along side. Or, he hid them elsewhere, in a spot too good for the L.E. officers to find. Now, they were completing the routine safety inspection, and they would be leaving within the next three hours or so.

*My taxpayer dollars at work*, she thought cynically, taking a draw from her cigar.

Jay, an MK2 from A-gang, walked out from the back of the helo hanger and stood beside the trashcan. He didn't talk much, but he wasn't unfriendly--it was just his way. She also knew he was on the initial boarding team.

"Hey, Jay. How was it out there?"

Jay smirked, not taking his eyes off the freighter. "It was all right."

"Did you go into the engine room?"

Jay glanced at her. "Nah." He flashed his shy grin. "It was boring."

She smiled back at him. "I don't know how y'all do it. There's no way I'd volunteer for this shit."

"Ah, it's not so bad." He looked out at the water and shrugged. "It's something to do," he added.

"Still." She shook her head and smirked. "I figured out a long time ago I belonged in the rear with the gear. No way I could do that."

◆ ◆ ◆ ◆

*The Suburbs of Albany, NY;*
*Three days before Infusion*

In a room with the curtains drawn, keeping the horrors in and the sunshine out, a tiny body lay shallowly breathing on a bed in the center of the room. It lay encased in brightly-colored dinosaur sheets and a The Solar System bedspread, reminders of the child that it once was. A child who was a seven-year-old boy who once followed the Yankees, and was young enough to believe that his Dad was the greatest man who ever lived.

The body belonged to a boy once, but the essence of the boy did not seem to dwell there anymore. The belt restraints had rubbed the boy's wrists and ankles raw. In the early days of his illness, he would strain against them as he thrashed around the bed. These days he still growled, he still screamed, but he mostly slept. Or, it looked like slumber--his eyelids never throbbed with the signs of REM sleep. The body was still battling to survive, but lately it had been losing its ground.

The doctors had examined him, done blood tests, even managed an MRI, but they had come up with nothing. Even though the child had degraded to an infantile state, not able to feed himself or even control his bowels, there was nothing wrong with the boy physically.

The doctors were perplexed. The best diagnosis they could come up with was that it was some sort of acute psychosis. They wanted to hospitalize the child but his parents refused, hiring three nurses to care for him at home instead. Medications had been administered but, the doctors warned, it could take time to find the right balance.

Once they diagnosed the problem, though, they were confident they could come up with a treatment plan.

His home life appeared to be as stable as they came, so they had quickly ruled out abuse. The boy came from a two-parent household, with one little brother. Looking around his room, one could tell he was once a happy little kid. He was in Little League: his ball and glove was on a shelf, now collecting dust. Boy Scout paraphernalia was scattered around the room, and pictures of him with his family were on the wall: fishing trips, attending baseball games. All smiles and freckles.

Nothing like the tiny framework of bones and skin that lay on the bed now. Tubes protruded from everywhere: a tube to feed him, a tube to hydrate him, tubes to carry away the body's wastes. He was motionless on the bed. Maybe he was dreaming, but who knew?

His parents looked much older now. His mother was near collapse after

8

six weeks of watching her firstborn deteriorate and enduring the daily struggles of washing and changing both children, even with help. The father wasn't doing well, either; he had been spending more time in the office over the past week, trying to catch up on work fallen behind, and trying to ignore what was happening to his son. Slowly but surely, he was working on becoming a stranger.

It had all started late one night. The parents had awoken to screaming, objects breaking, and feet running up the steps. They got up and put their robes on, but they didn't start to run until they heard a second scream accompany the first. They heard the sound of glass breaking.

By the time they got to the baby's room, they saw in the moonlight their oldest son with his baseball bat, making no sound. In his left hand, he had his baby brother by the ankle. The little one was bruised and a little bloody from being pulled over the guard rail and onto the floor, but he was alive--and screaming his head off. Glass from the window above covered the floor in jagged pieces, blood coated the bat, and a couple dark wet globules dropped onto the carpet.

Josh was still screaming. The older brother turned to look at him, and then raised the bat. Just in time, the father tackled his son and grabbed the child before the bat came down onto the baby's head.

Their eldest son wouldn't be calmed. They carried him back to his room, and he thrashed around on the bed, trying to bite, to scratch--trying to get away. Finally, the parents had to use the long sleeves from his little shirts to secure the child to the bed so they could check the rest of the house and call the doctor.

On the other side of the house, the remains of the cat were spattered against the wall. Furniture was broken, pillows were slashed, and feathers thrown everywhere. Every kitchen knife was on the floor.

As time passed, the tubes began to appear. The child had lost his ability to function for himself. He wouldn't eat, and would try to bite anyone who would try to feed him. It became a nightmare.

Of course, relatives had been by and called from time to time to help and offer support. But the mother was side-swiped by the phone call from her great aunt on her mother's side.

"You can't be serious, Aunt Cathy."

"Sweetheart, I know you and Mac aren't religious. God knows we all got so worried when you turned away from the Church..."

"Aunt Cathy..." The mother interrupted, sighing; she was too tired for this.

"Honey, just...would you consider the idea? I mean, what would it hurt to have a priest look at him?"

The mother was trying to remain calm. *Are you effing serious?*

"Because this isn't the movies, that's why! Things like that don't happen. My son isn't...!"

"How do you know?" Aunt Cathy interrupted. "People don't talk about it 'cause they're so quick to blame it on a medical problem, or throw pills at it. None of the young people go to Church anymore...the doctors don't know, do they? I don't know if Father Calhoun would travel all the way up there, but I'm sure he knows a very nice priest that would come up..."

"No--no, Aunt Cathy. I'll find one around here." *Anything to end this conversation...*

Still, after hanging up a few minutes later, the mother hesitated. It was ludicrous, right? It wasn't the goddamn Dark Ages...

But, as she went back upstairs and gazed on her firstborn, she knew that love overrode logic and reason. In another day or two, she would have to put her son in the hospital, and she did not want him to die there. And, the desperate often find themselves doing things they never dreamed they would do, under normal circumstances.

She went to the phone book, and looked under "Churches, Catholic."

*The Caribbean Sea:*

The fantail erupted with the roar of a P-250 dewatering pump. The Damage Controlman and the Machinery Technician running the pump checked the discharge psi, the oil, and the fuel lines. They had to nurse the fuel a little by pumping the priming bulb, but that was normal. They opened up the fire nozzle, and water spewed out over the side. They'd let it run a couple of minutes more, and then they could pack up and call it a day.

They vaguely heard the creak of the watertight door opening over the noise, and both looked up to see another DC wander out.

The two men looked at each other. They both rolled their eyes and went back to checking the engine.

The other DC went over and looked at the engine. She started to yell something.

The DC ignored her. The MK followed suit. She kept yelling.

Finally, the DC throttled down the engine.

"TURN IT OFF!" The female shouted. "TURN IT OFF!"

One of them turned it to "Off." The engine died.

"You didn't have water in your discharge," the female DC said. "Something's wrong. It'll burn up."

"It runs," he shrugged. Then they turned their backs on her and began to drain the pump.

Frustrated, the female turned and went back inside. She went straight to the DC Shop, and found the DC1.

"Dan, will you tell those dickhead assholes that if there isn't water in the discharge, they'll burn out the P-250?"

"Why didn't you tell them that?"

"I did. They didn't listen."

Dan turned and looked at her. Then he looked up at a point on the ceiling and twitched his mouth.

"All right, I'll take care of it." He edged past her and left the shop, traveling aft.

The female was left alone in the DC shop. It wasn't the first time something like that had happened.

◆  ◆  ◆  ◆

*Albany, NY:*

Father Roberts enjoyed the life of a priest in 21st century suburbia. When he had taken over the parish of St. John the Baptist twenty years before, he was dedicated to becoming a beacon for the community. He would resurrect the congregation, start outreach programs, and comfort the suffering masses, looking for hope.

10

And while he had done quite a bit for the local community over the years, it was a rather affluent suburb, and he had found his comfortable niche a long time ago. He presided over weddings, funerals, and christenings. He counseled the newly engaged and aided seasoned couples riding marital storms. He comforted the grieving. It had all become wonderfully routine.

So, one can imagine his reaction to the strange phone call he received that Tuesday afternoon, with an even stranger request. He listened and asked questions for clarification.

No, she assured him, this wasn't a prank.

No, the doctors couldn't find anything physically wrong with the child.

Yes, she was brought up in the Catholic faith, but her family didn't go to Mass. Her children weren't even baptized.

No, she wasn't really interested in coming to Church, but would he consider coming down to the house? She wasn't sure how long her son could hang on.

After he hung up, Father Roberts thought about that poor family. He was familiar with the ritual she mentioned, but he hadn't had any experience with exorcism since they taught a lesson about it at the seminary. Most normal people didn't ask for something like that, not in this day and age--even if they did think it was a possibility. But, he had noticed a renewed interest such things lately. All of those horror movies…

*She must be desperate…poor child…*

He never actually agreed to the exorcism. Unlike what people see in the movies, the ritual takes several hours and should be done with more than one person. You need approval. You need priests who are specially trained. And, it is sloppy. At his age, Father Roberts was not into sloppy. He sympathized with the mother but, what this situation seemed to call for at this time was comfort, and a reminder of God's love for all His children. Not a long, involved process that would probably just upset the child and the parents. No, he decided, a simple blessing and anointing with oil would be sufficient. If the situation presented itself that a true exorcism is needed, he could begin the process in short time.

That Friday afternoon, the priest packed a Bible, a crucifix, a vial of oil, pamphlets about St. John church, and his wallet in his folding black bag. So armed to do battle with the unknown, he drove his 1992 Chevy station wagon to the house on Rodin Street, where all the troubles began.

11

# ·CHAPTER TWO·

*Suburbs of Albany, NY*
*Infusion, Day 0:*

"Hello, Father Roberts. Thank you for coming." The door was opened by a tired-looking woman in jeans and a NYU sweatshirt. She stepped aside to let him into the house.

"God bless all in this house," Father Roberts pronounced the old Irish blessing that he liked to say as he stepped though the doorway. He removed his hat and looked around the living room. It was clean, comfortable. It was decorated in a contemporary Asian style, and there were a few expensive-looking swords on the walls.

*Encased in glass*, Father Roberts noted. *Good idea, with young ones in the house.*

A baby was standing up in a playpen, holding on to the edge, rocking back and forth. He gave the child a grin, and received a gummy grin in return.

"That's Josh, Tim's little brother. Mac will be home soon." The mother gestured to the sofa. "Would you like something to drink?"

"Thank you, no. Actually, I'd like to get started. Let me see the boy, and then we can talk."

"Of course." The mother turned and started up the stairs. "This way."

The priest followed the mother up the stairs and down a small, dark hallway. At the end of the corridor, she opened a door and walked into a darker room.

She turned on a table lamp, and the priest crossed himself at the sight of the thin body nestled in the bed. The boy's hair was thin, and the eyes were sunken into his face. He appeared to be sleeping. Thin transparent tubing protruded from underneath the bedclothes. There were restraints available on the bed, but Tim wasn't bound at the moment.

"Hello, Tim," he whispered. *God help this child.*

He started to sit down on the bed, but the mother grabbed his arm.

"Be very careful, Father. He sleeps most of the time these days, but when he's awake..." Her voice broke, and pain crossed over her face. She looked over at her son helplessly. "He's mean," she finished.

"Of course." He shifted his body and sat instead on a chair next to the bed. He opened his black bag and began to rummage for the cross. He kissed it as he took it out of the bag, and set it on the bed. He also took out the oil vial and Bible.

A wail from downstairs broke the silence.

"That's Josh. Will you be OK, Father?"

"Sure. Go ahead."

The mother hurried out of the room.

Father Roberts turned to Tim. He didn't want to wake the child needlessly, though he couldn't see why the child was doing so poorly. It was like the child was pining away.

The priest stood and crossed the air beside the child. He began a time-honored invocation as he reached for the oil.

The boy opened his eyes and looked at him.

"Well, hello Tim. I'm Father Roberts. I hear you haven't been feeling well," Father Roberts said in his most soothing voice.

Tim didn't say anything in return, but stared at the priest with empty eyes. He didn't move. Then he closed his eyes, and sighed.

The priest unscrewed the vial, and tipped the vessel so some oil wet his thumb. He reached across the boy's body, bending down to anoint the child's forehead with oil.

"Timothy, I bless thee..." Out of the corner of his eye he noticed the child's lips were cracked and blood was oozing across his mouth.

"In the name of the Father..." He made the sign of the cross on the child's forehead, and then tipped the vial again for more oil.

"And of the Son..." Tim's eyes opened, but Father Roberts didn't notice. His eyes were on the vial and his thumb as he tipped it once more and reached down.

"And of the Holy..."

The boy's head whipped up, and to the priest's horror, the child clamped down on his hand.

Father Roberts cried out as the boy's teeth cut through his hand. He felt his hand get wet, he felt dizzy, and he saw a flash of light...

Timmy felt nauseous, sick, and weak. He remembered some sort of tunnel, a light, and now he was in his bed, but...why did he feel so weak? He blinked his eyes and looked at an old man in a dark suit. The stranger looked as confused as Timmy felt.

"Who are you?"

The old man stared at him. Then Timmy noticed the strange white collar around the man's neck. Where had he seen that...?

"Oh! You're a pastor." Timmy felt a little calmer. Mom said pastors were good people.

"Your hand is bleeding." Timmy licked his cracked lips--blood. Had he bitten the pastor? "Where's my Mom?"

The priest looked like he was thinking about something. He walked around the room, looking at his hands and muttering to himself.

Suddenly, the man looked up, around the room, then at Timmy. Timmy thought he might be trying to smile, but it looked more like showing teeth. He started to get scared again.

"Mister?" he croaked nervously. He looked toward the doorway. "Mommy?" he called weakly.

The man reached down and touched his cheek. Then he brought the bleeding hand to Timmy's mouth.

Timmy tasted the blood and, sickened, squirmed to get away. He felt dizzy; saw a flash of light...

*Back here.* The first soul murmured, looking through the boy's eyes at the priest. The man grinned.

*Yes!* The second soul replied. The two of them were sharing the boy's body. The third soul was still in the priest's body.

*Will go to him.* The first motioned to the third to release the boy from his bonds. Once he was free, the first raised the boy's arm and grabbed the man's hand, and raised it to the boy's mouth. The second coursed his spirit through the blood of the boy, out the lips, and into the man. He sensed the spirit of the other.

*Their blood--carries us.*

*Yes!*

*Need more sharp things...* The second looked around, and then saw a small object on the dresser. He searched the man's mind...

13

*"Swiss Knife"...very sharp!* He projected his thoughts to the first demon. *Get the knife, and then call the woman.*

The boy's body arose from the bed, reached over, and the first took the blade. The first had no idea how the humans managed to communicate with their mouths--"talking", they called it, with only one soul--but he knew how to make the woman run to him.

*I did not know this about their blood,* the third said.

*Could we be the first?* The first couldn't believe it.

*I have never heard of this. We will ask the others.*

*Ready?* the first asked the other souls.

The priest nodded.

The first fumbled with the knife but finally unfolded it and calmly cut the priest's arm. Blood flowed. The second and the third felt the pain, but it was mild. In fact, compared to the numbness of where they had been, it was an almost delicious sensation. They got behind the door.

The first took a breath and let out a shriek. Then they all paused.

"Father Roberts?" they heard her call. They listened as the footfalls thumped up the stairs. "Father Roberts?" The woman ran into the room.

The mother saw her son, awake, standing by the foot of the bed. She didn't see Father Roberts.

"What's going on?" she gasped.

The second and the third stepped behind the woman and spun her around by the arm, so she faced them.

As she stepped back from the priest, the boy cut her arm.

She recoiled from the pain and screamed as she saw her blood spurt out. Then she saw Father Roberts grab her arm and press it to his.

A second later, the second was looking through the mother's eyes.

*We need to call the others,* the first told his brothers. *Tell them...*

The third nodded. The priest looked blankly at the wall for a full minute, and then turned to look at his brothers.

*They're coming. We need more sharp things--knives.*

The second searched the mother's mind. *Many, many sharp things down the steps. "Knives" and "Swords!"*

The first paused. He looked down at the boy's body. *This human is dying. I need another body soon.*

The third suddenly felt the presence of more souls, right on the fringe of this dimension, asking to come into the priest with him. He made room, and twenty more demons came into the body.

*Greetings.* The third felt closed in and was rapidly becoming irritable, being crammed in one body with twenty other souls, but it was so much easier to possess a body whose soul has already been made dormant. Plus, with their combined power, they could control the body better.

*Greetings.* A fourth spoke for them. *We are ready.*

*We will find bodies for each of you. It is time to live!*

A moment later, a door opened downstairs. A voice called out.

"Honey!" The door slammed shut.

"Hi, Josh!" A pause.

"Honey? Are you upstairs?"

The first looked in the boy's mind. He smiled. *"Dad!"*

He handed the knife to the second and started for the doorway. The woman palmed the knife and, growling happily, she followed her son into the hallway to meet her husband.

14

# ·CHAPTER THREE·

*Philadelphia, PA*
*Two Days after Infusion*

"Everyone must remain calm! Please go to your homes! That is the safest place!"

Sergeant Michael Beal lowered the loudspeaker and looked at the destruction surrounding him. He was on top of a tank, fully decked in riot gear. The tank was slowly making its way down Broad Street, again, running over cars that had already been crushed hours ago. He was standing in the top porthole, watching as people ran like water around the tank and went--who knew where? They probably didn't even know where...

Fires were burning, homes were smoldering, and gunshots rang out in the distance. Sirens were blaring all over the city, and hospitals were standing room only.

*At least in Los Angeles the rioting was isolated to a few neighborhoods*, he thought. *This is too damn much for us to handle...*

The National Guard was called twenty-four hours ago by Governor Denjison to calm the citizens and maybe get some order in the major cities in Pennsylvania. So far, all they've managed to do is look impressive, run over some cars with their tanks, and keep City Hall from burning to the ground. No reports of the virus had been reported in the city so far, but it was heading this way. Like swarms of locusts, the mobs had started in New York and were spreading in all directions. Beal could almost empathize with the scared people of Philadelphia. The Infected were mindless, hungry, and, in a word, sick.

He had acquired and read the final reports last night from the National Guard in New York City before it had been completely overrun and they had to pull out. Any "well people" still left up there could only look forward to gang rapes, torture, starvation...and that's if they weren't run to death by the virus. Corpses were everywhere, rotting where they lay. There weren't even enough people left to bury the dead. It was complete desolation.

*And now it's spreading here. Except you won't need the Infected to destroy this town. The "well" people will do it for them...*

Beal wiped his brow and tried to fight the nausea that had been slowly building all day. He wasn't fooled by the morning pep-talk the command gave this morning. Those last reports were not for the enlisted to read, but they got filtered down anyway. The officers spoke of The City of Brotherly Love being the "Line Drawn in the Sand--Here and No Further." (Captain Fuller often conversed in capital letters, even casually.) The captain spoke of the National Guard taking a "Last Stand" here in Philadelphia, that even without "Federal Aid" the mobs would be subdued at the city limits, and the Infected Would Be Captured And Held At Bay Until They Could Be Cured! Boo-yah!

*Boo-yah. Yeah...*

What got to Sergeant Beal most was the lack of federal military response. Not one marine had reported to help them, not one Army grunt was in sight. It was as if all of the guys with the fucking money just--disappeared. Sure, he had seen a few rioters in uniform, but they seemed lost. Swanson had heard that the military bases and installations were locked down tight. No one got in or out, unless they requested it.

Beal decided to give up reasoning with the good people of Philadelphia and crawled down the ladder, shutting the scuttle above him and locking it down. He settled down in a chair and sighed. It was getting dark, anyway.

"This is bullshit, Kill. Let's go back to base. I want to see my wife." All the families had been moved to temporary quarters on the Guard base last night when the troops had been recalled.

"You've got it, Sarge." The tank was slow, and they were confined to the major streets, so it would take a while.

About ten minutes into the ride home, Swanson gave a shout. He had been looking through the periscope and navigating.

"One of ours is out there! He's been hurt! I think it's Allen."

Beal looked through the periscope. There was one man, in uniform, lying in the center of the road, bleeding. He looked as though he was unconscious.

"Fuck." He paused, and then made a command decision. "OK, let's grab him."

The tank came to a halt, and Beal climbed up the ladder to the scuttle. He looked over his shoulder to Swanson.

"Radio base what I'm doing. Cover me. Anything weird happens, leave us. OK, Swanson? Killark?"

"Yeah, Sarge."

Beal felt really creepy about this. Allen was not a friend, but he was a soldier.

*Probably got hurt by rioters, the bastards.*

He opened the scuttle, climbed out, and shut the scuttle behind him. Crouching down on top of the tank, rifle in hand, he looked around. Surprisingly, no people (insane or otherwise) were on this street at this moment. Except for Allen.

"Allen!" he called out. The soldier didn't respond. Beal climbed down the tank's outside ladder and carefully approached the prone figure on the ground. Allen seemed to be twitching slightly, and there was a little blood around his mouth, but no wounds.

*Oh, God.* Beal felt ill, and knew something wasn't right. He couldn't explain it, but it was just--something felt wrong about Allen. He was about to turn around and go back when Allen groaned.

"Allen?" Beal was now standing next to the soldier. He ripped off his glove and started to bend down to check his pulse. His thoughts pulsed and ran into a blur:

*Bad...this is bad-not-right. Not right! Get-up-get-out-of-here!*
*RUN!*
***RUN!***

Beal paused in mid-kneel and tensed his left thigh muscle to spring and run.

Allen jerked up and bit Beal's finger.

◆　◆　◆　◆

Considering the virus was up north, and in the big cities, this just didn't seem possible. Bobby Thacknay was being chased by his older brother. His brother that had slashed their parents and was now after him.

They were all eating dinner when Carl just fell to the floor. He was moaning. He was twitching. Ma and Pop bent over to help him, and the next thing he knew they were lying on the floor on either side of him, a huge red smile carved on each throat, blood pouring out. And Carl was covered with their blood, grinning.

And Bobby could feel it. It wasn't Carl.

Bob didn't even think after that. He ran. He ran out the door and into the barn. Thank God there was a 20 gauge shotgun there. His Pop had taught him how to use it just last year on his 14th birthday.

*Pop...*

Bobby tried not to think about him. He'd break down and cry if he did, and now he had more important things to do. He had to get away, and he knew if his brother found him, he would kill Bobby.

And he needed to kill Carl first.

No one knew that much about the virus, but it was transmitted by blood. And the people that were sick traveled in packs, and ran and murdered and did all kinds of bad stuff until their bodies wore out and they died.

There was no cure. There was no treatment. All they could do is shoot the Infected--and shoot to kill.

*How the hell did Carl get sick so quick? There wasn't anyone around, for Christ's sake!*

Bobby ran up the steps of the barn and into the hayloft. There was a little moonlight pouring through the slats in the walls, but it was mostly dark. He opened the shotgun and checked the cylinders.

*Shit. Shit, shit, shit!*

*Jesus, how could he have been so* stupid*?!*

No shot. He'd have to go back down and grab some from the box on the counter.

Terror seized him. He felt his heart pound in his chest and his breath quickened. He felt his dinner push up his throat.

*Now I know what a deer must feel like.*

He clicked the gun shut and felt for the first wooden rung with his foot. He found it and put weight on it. It creaked, and he listened for noises below.

The cows were thumping around down there, and he heard the wind whistling through the slats in the wall, but nothing unusual. He started down the ladder.

He stopped halfway down to listen. Nothing. OK so far.

He reached the bottom and ran for the table. He got there and grabbed a handful of shells.

*God, where the hell was Carl?*

That's when he heard the barn door creak. Just a little, but just enough.

*Load the gun or run? Load the gun or run?* He decided. He opened the gun and loaded two shells.

Out of the corner of his eye, in the light of a dying sun, he saw a dark form slinking along the back wall. The moonlight glinted on something shiny and metallic.

No--now it was starting to run. Right towards him. He slammed the chambers home and pointed the shotgun at Carl.

Suddenly, it hit him that, even though he was infected, it was Carl. The guy that taught him to shoot baskets. Who gave him noogies that didn't hurt. The only brother he had.

Bobby decided. He aimed for Carl's knee and fired. Carl fell to the ground screaming.

Bobby cautiously approached the howling figure on the dirt floor.

"OH, JESUS!" Carl shouted. "What the hell did you do that for?" He clutched at his knee. "AHHHHHHH!"

"Carl?" Bobby still had the muzzle trained at Carl's head. "How do I know it's you?"

Carl was panting, trying to stay conscious. "What the fuck, Bobby? It's me!" He paused a second, realizing he wasn't in the dining room; he didn't know how he got in the barn. His eyes widened.

"What happened, Bobby?"

Bobby didn't move. He aimed the shotgun at Carl's head. "Where do you keep Dad's old Hustlers?"

"What?"

"Where do you keep your damn Hustlers?"

Carl groaned in agony. "What the fuck, Dipshit, in that tin box... Ahhhh!... underneath a floorboard in my room, fuckin' a'!" He panted. "What the fuck? You're scaring me, Bobby! Where's Ma and Pop?"

Bobby lowered his rifle. He felt his defenses lower, and tears filled his eyes.

He didn't know what was there before, but it was Carl now.

"You were sick, Carl. You had the virus, and..."

He choked on his words. He couldn't continue. What could he say? He forced reality from his mind and focused on the practical. His brother was hurt. His brother needed him now.

"Let's get you to the hospital. I'll explain on the way."


*Portsmouth, VA*
*Six Hours Later*

"Hurry up, man! They're gaining on us!"

In the dead of night, two men were running for their lives down a twisting road. They had been hiding out in their apartment, but they had run out of food two days ago. They hoped there would be refuge at the Coast Guard base--if they could only get there. They had been holed up only fifteen minutes away--walking distance--and there was no moon...they thought they had a chance.

But the mob had been in the trees, waiting. And not just for them.

The air was filled with a horrible sweet smell, making it hard for the two men to breathe. As they ran, sometimes they felt the dirt beneath them squish, and they had to leap over longish obstacles in the road, but they didn't have time to think about that at the moment.

As long as they didn't become a longish obstacle in the road themselves, they would be fine.

Only problem was, the mob was chasing them now. About twenty of the Infected, carrying axes, knives--whatever they could find that was sharp. They thought they recognized several of the possessed as Coasties from other ships. Hell, some might be from the *Dispatch*, it didn't matter now. Now, they had to get behind

18

the fence.

They saw the lights of the base in the distance. The city electricity went out about four days ago, when the mobs took over. The base had guns and generators, and a chain-link fence with barbed-wire over the top. It was the perfect place to hide.

Matt turned as he ran and fired his .45 indiscriminately into the crowd behind them. He was low on ammo, but at this point, who gave a fuck? Of course, the mob didn't care in the least. They kept chasing them. And somehow catching up.

"We're almost there!" Brydan pumped his arms and sprinted towards the gate. The gate was closed, but there were two men guarding it. They both wore respirators.

"For God's sake! We're coasties! Help us!" Brydan screamed ahead.

The guards paused, and then one of them went to the gate.

"Oh, thank God," Matt panted, not breaking stride. "We're going to make it!"

One of the guards had an M-16. When Matt and Brydan were at 100 yards, the guard began firing at the mob. Bullets whizzed past Matt and Bryan's ears, and they heard the animals behind them screaming and grunting, and the thumps as they fell.

In the floodlights of the base, Brydan could see blood and bodies everywhere. He thought he saw bullet holes in some of them. Brydan had been slowly pulling ahead of Matt, and was a good twenty yards ahead of him when he approached the gate. The gate was opened, and Brydan rushed through. He whipped around, a huge grin spreading across his face, to welcome his friend to safety.

His smile vanished as he heard the guard fire his weapon, and saw Matt crumple to the ground, screaming. The mob was upon him a second later, slicing him apart with their knives. There was blood, and ripping --then Matt was quiet. Brydan heard the gate click shut.

Brydan was still in shock as he watched the mob suddenly stop and get deathly silent. They all straightened up in one motion and looked across the fence. The two border guards raised their M-16s and aimed them in challenge. The mob turned, and calmly walked back towards the woods and the night. Matt's body lay with the rest of the corpses.

The guards turned to him. He recognized one of them beneath his mask as a GM2 from the cutter Point Charge. He was the one that spoke, and spoke carefully, deliberately.

"Your friend had to be a diversion, Brydan. He was too close to the mob, and they would have gotten through. We can't allow that. And...I didn't recognize him."

"He was my roommate, you Motherfucker," Brydan growled, his voice starting to rise. He took a step forward and would have said more, but at that moment a sharp pain erupted from the back of his head, and everything went black. He slumped to the ground.

"You're fuckin' welcome," the other guard named Hirsht answered, standing over Brydan, still grasping the rifle in his two hands, the butt pointing down.

"Call Security, Swift." Hirsht glanced at him, lowering his rifle. He blinked. "What? He was about to get violent, you know that."

"Yeah," Swift answered, sighing. He slung his rifle over his shoulder and walked to the guard's shack. Swift pulled his respirator aside and took a breath

19

through his nose.  He gagged.  He picked up the phone receiver and punched four numbers.  He switched to breathing through his mouth.

"Yeah, this is GM2 Swift.  We have another one that made it.  MK-something Brydan Townsend.  You know him?"

A pause.  "Yeah, he's off the *Dispatch*."  He listened for several more seconds.

"Right."  He hung up and turned to Hirsht.  "They're taking him to the clinic, I guess."

Hirsht shrugged and looked at the unconscious body.  "Where else?"

# ◆CHAPTER FOUR◆

*Kline Federal Laboratories*
*Outside Bel Air, Maryland*
*Five Days after Infusion*

With the exception of key local officials who were paid very well, no one in Bel Air knew about Kline Federal Laboratories. And for good reason: viral infections were tested there. The really deadly ones. Deadly enough that, if airborne, they could easily wipe out the town and spread to Baltimore in a matter of days. And from Baltimore to the rest of the country. And probably, from there, the world.

So, the less the public knew about this facility, the happier everyone was.

Dr. Marge Patterson, a graduate of Johns Hopkins (twice) and the youngest on staff, thought this infection sweeping the country was a virus. Certainly, they had bugs that contagious in stock. Plus, the virus started in Albany, NY, where Warren Federal Laboratories was quietly nestled in a docile suburb, underneath an ordinary-looking shopping mall. No one had heard from the lab, and it was widely assumed in her circles it had started there.

Marge peered into a microscope and studied the few drops of blood underneath the lens. Nothing unusual. She sat up and took off her glasses, which were always getting fogged up from her breathing into her surgical mask. She fumbled around the tabletop for a tissue to wipe them off.

The sample was taken from a man--if you wanted to call the subject that-- who was captured in Baltimore. After two of the six federal agents lost their lives in the reconnaissance mission, the man was found in a building, alone, happily ripping his teeth into the leg of a woman he had raped not too long before that.

Charitably, one of the agents had fired a mercy shot between the woman's eyes before they captured the man. Marge still shivered when she thought about that. The woman, however, seemed clean of the infection.

Strange thing, that, she contemplated as she found a tissue and began to rub her glasses. Women were more likely to be torture and rape victims, but were not as susceptible to the virus as men. Then again, there were plenty of women who were infected. Viruses never discriminated between genders, but who was to say this wasn't engineered somehow? But that was beyond the lab's technology, certainly.

But, on this slide, there were no viruses. Perfectly healthy blood. She didn't get it.

She put her glasses back on and slid off her stool. The lab was painted white, with harsh white florescent lights hanging off the ceiling. It was efficient and sterile and had as much character as an aspirin pill. Still, it was the place she called home for two years, and Marge did not mind it much. As drab as it was, Marge would have much rather had money put into her lab supplies than some soothing green paint and pictures. Even though she was only 28, she was very old for her age. She had seen a lot.

Marge cleaned up her station, got rid of the biohazard material, and opened the door into the outer vestibule. The positive air pressure made her ears pop. The door closed, and she began to strip her paper outfit, as per federal biohazard protocols.

There was talk that the scientists were about to be moved. Though the virus hadn't infiltrated too many small communities like Bel Air yet, the virus was almost non-existent in the Midwest. Certainly, considering what was here, it was better to get the scientists to safety and close up shop than to have the doctors go mad and start breaking bottles of world-enders 'cause they made neat tinkly sounds.

She finished removing her suit and shoved all the textured white paper into the trash chute. Opening her mouth, she opened the second door to the outside corridor. The positive pressure popped her ears again, and she stepped through the doorway and started down the passageway, to visit her patient.

At the end of the hall to the right, in a darkened room, a man that once must have been incredibly attractive lay unmoving on the bed. He had short black hair and green eyes and, until he became infected, was a social worker for the City of Baltimore. It was proof that the virus corrupted the mind absolutely, in her opinion. During his stay at Kline he was sedated, of course, and was rarely awake. During those times when he was restrained and was allowed to awaken, it was all garbled nonsense. They would ask him questions, but he wouldn't answer any of them.

They were planning to wake him up one more time. After that, he would be transferred to a military facility in Wyoming. Who knew how--everything was chaos out there--but they seemed sure of themselves.

*The same way they're getting us out, Marge,* she chastised herself. *However that is...*

The patient, who was known as George B. Weaver before he became sick, moaned. She visually checked that the wrist and ankle bands were in place, and walked to the side of the bed.

"George?" she asked in a soft voice. "George, are you there?"

George moaned and tried to raise his arms. When he couldn't get them up more than a few inches he tried again, with more force. His moans became grunts.

"George, I'm Dr. Patterson, and I'm here to help you." George opened his eyes and stared at her breasts.

*Great,* she thought dryly. *This is progress...*

"Can you tell me how you're feeling?" George drooled onto his chest.

Marge sighed and left the room to tell a nurse that the patient was awake.

A few minutes later, Dr. Lee Timachi was gingerly checking George's pulse while the patient pulled on the restraints violently.

"94, I think--so far, so good," he said to the nurse, who was a big man with ebony skin that everyone called Tiny. "He seems strong enough, though he's rapidly lost muscle tone in the past two days. Very weird."

The nurse wrote the number down on the chart. "Y'know," Tiny said hesitantly. "This whole thing reminds me of a Bible story. Did you go to church as a kid, Dr. Timachi?"

"No, my parents were Buddhists. But, I had a girlfriend that took me to a Methodist church for a while." Dr. Timachi grinned. "Why do you ask?"

"One of the things Jesus did while he was on Earth was exorcise demons. Y'know, cast them out?"

Dr. Timachi looked at Tiny with a lot of skepticism. "You're kidding, right?"

Tiny shook his head. "Nope. The way he's thrashing around and moaning--just like demons."

"So, what do you recommend, we call a priest?"

"Well," Tiny began. "Isn't one of the guys who knows about us a reverend?"

An hour later, Dr. Morgan Bartholomew of the Bel Air Church of Christ and a long-standing member of the city council was driven by special invitation to the lab. Though Lee Timachi came to visit from time to time, Morgan had visited the lab only once before, when it was first built. There had never been a need to go back until now.

He was one of the council members on the lab's special payroll. Over the years he had made sure every penny of his bribe money went to the church and the community. Anonymously, of course. He was pretty sure the other members who were paid off kept the money for themselves, but Morgan never felt right about that. As it was, he slept soundly every night, and he hoped his fellow members could say the same.

Well, almost every night. Sometimes he would lie awake in his bed, considering the deal he had made with the devil. He tried not to dwell on the time bomb ticking in their midst, deep in the ground. But, he would reason to himself, the government probably would have built there with or without council approval, so might as well play nice...

When the driver had found him, he was sitting in his office as he usually would on a Tuesday. Hell was coming to them all, but he was reminded the old story of the farmer who, though warned to flee, kept to his fields as the floodwaters surged to drown him, because he felt that was the best thing to do. When the virus came for him, it would find him at his plow.

"Parishioners might come in," Morgan complained to the driver as he pulled on his coat. "What's so important?"

"Can't say," the man replied. In a three-piece black suit and a buzz haircut, he looked like a man who didn't take no for an answer. "Might want to take some supplies."

Morgan went still and looked up at the driver. "Supplies?"

The driver shrugged. "The doc said something about bringing holy water and a cross."

"OK..." Morgan went around to the bookshelf behind his desk and grabbed a wooden cross on a gold chain and a plastic bottle of holy water. "Sure you can't tell me what this is about?" the pastor asked, pocketing the items.

"Can't say," the driver repeated. "We need to go."

Lee Timachi was waiting for him at the front door as they pulled up. The scientist explained the situation as they walked into the building and down the main hall.

Morgan stopped in his tracks. "You can't be serious."

Lee shrugged. "Look, I don't believe in demons, or angels for that matter, but Tiny--I mean Nurse Clark--seems to think it's worth you taking a look."

Morgan smirked slightly. "You always listen to your nurses, Lee?"

Lee grinned back. "Well, usually I tend to listen to nurses that are a lot thinner and prettier, and have different plumbing, but I figured at worst you could provide spiritual comfort to Mr. Weaver."

"Very well." Morgan started down the hall again, but stopped three steps later. "What do you know about this...condition? No one seems to know anything in the press."

"Not airborne yet. Right now, it's purely blood-to-blood transfer, so stay away from his mouth. Mr. Weaver is restrained and poses no threat to anyone--as long as he doesn't bite anyone--or you bleed all over him."

Morgan gave him a sideways glance.

Lee continued. "He gets weaker by the day, like he's wasting away. He's getting fed plenty by tube, so we don't know what's going on. He's irrational to say the least...we found him in a cannibalistic act."

Morgan stared at Lee. "My God..."

"Yeah," Lee replied. They both stood by a doorway. "He's here."

Morgan walked into the simple white room and stood by the foot of the bed. He took the bottle and the cross out of his pocket and laid them on the nightstand. Weaver opened his eyes and looked at the pastor.

"Well," Morgan said, looking at Lee. "If he is possessed, we'll know in a minute. Though, far be it from me to argue with the conclusions of the US government."

After a short silent prayer, Morgan opened the vial and tipped it so water spread on his thumb. He made the sign of the cross on Weaver's forehead and jerked his hand back as Weaver snapped his jaws towards his fingers.

"No you don't!" the pastor said, smiling.

His smile dropped as he saw wisps of smoke rising from the moist cross he had just made.

*No shit...*

Morgan got nervous, but he bore down.

"I command you, in the name of Jesus Christ, tell me your name!" Weaver started to wail and thrash about. The pastor felt adrenaline start to kick in.

"The power of Christ compels you, Spirit of Darkness! In the name of Jesus, I command you to leave this body!" The wails became screams.

*God help me, this might be for real!* Morgan thought. He suddenly was seized with fear. He fought the primal urge to run.

"Tell me your name!" He shook the vial once, and a stream of water droplets landed on Weaver.

The wet skin smoked.

"Tell me your name!" He shook again.

The skin began to bubble.

Then, in the next moment, Morgan felt his fear pass from him as he found courage in the rightness of God and his proclamations of faith.

"IN THE NAME OF CHRIST, DEMON! TELL ME YOUR NAME!"

Weaver threw his head back, screamed, then looked at the pastor with hate-filled eyes.

"We," George Weaver spat, in a gravelly voice that came straight from Hell, "are Legion. For we...are Many..."

# ✦CHAPTER FIVE✦

*Off Port Hattaras, NC*
*Six Days after Infusion*

DC2 Townsend , Elizabeth J.; 212-34-8563; stared at the sea, leaning against the rail on the flight deck of the *Surveyor* (WMEC 915), feeling the breeze press against her, and dreamed of her husband--and of going home.  She had three days left of this patrol, and her patience was rewarded by watching the sea in the last few days turn from the brilliant blue of the Caribbean to the darker, duller blue of the Eastern US Seaboard: they were on their way home.  Three more days, and she could walk off this pig and never look back, Thank God.  She was "short": her bags were already packed.  She would only ask Claire for a ride to her car when they pulled in and liberty was granted, and then she would start the 11-hour journey to her husband, who had served on another 270 in Virginia.  She had served her time in Hell, and she was ready to go.  Her future was in Virginia, and she couldn't wait to see him.

She met her husband three years ago when he was temporarily assigned to her first cutter.  FN Houston, Elizabeth J. was climbing up the ladder from the Engine Room of the *Buzzard Bay*, going to the Bridge to relieve the 0400-0800 inport watch.  The *Buzzard Bay* was an 140-foot ice breaking tugboat with detachable barge, stationed at the time in Portsmouth, VA.  As she looked up, she saw a guy she had never met before climbing down the ladder.  He was tall, with blond hair.  As they met midway, she could see his mellow grey-blue eyes and the third class crows glinting on his collar.  *Cute*, she thought to herself.  Lizzy wasn't sure if he was a new crewmember--dating shipmates was strictly against the rules--but, she decided to flirt a little as she arched her eyebrow and gave him a smile that she knew could draw male interest.

"Hi," she said.  "New here?"

"Yup."  He gave her the once-over.  "I'm Brydan.  I'm here until the *Dispatch* arrives.  The MAT said y'all needed help with your red gears."

*Ooh, "Y'all,"* Lizzy flushed with delight.  *Southern accent.  Even better...*

"MK1 is down below."

"Thanks."  Brydan kinda smiled a little, but looked a little wary.  "Who are you?"

"I'm FN Houston.  The guys in the Engine Room call me Lizzy."

Brydan nodded, a little distracted.  Lizzy had only been in the Coast Guard a year, but she could guess what he was thinking: *Whiner?  Morale Gear?  Maybe worth something?*

"OK.  See ya later."  He continued down the ladder.

Lizzy continued to the Bridge.  *OK... that was unimpressive*, she thought.

Once he saw that she was a hard worker and wasn't a doorknob (every guy gets a turn), they became friends, though casually.  Three months later she went to the DC-A school in Yorktown.  Even though Portsmouth was only 45 minutes away, she didn't come back to visit until she had her own set of crows.

Brydan was especially happy to see her.  Throughout her last evening in Portsmouth as Lizzy and her circle of friends went to the local Friendly's and a movie that was too stupid to remember, it seemed to Lizzy that Brydan was trying to keep Lizzy to himself. But, she dismissed this idea. She was on her way to the *Surveyor* in the morning--in Rhode Island. It's true, she often wondered what it would be like to kiss him and, damn, he did have a nice build but--c'mon, trying to date her now would be crazy...wouldn't it? Finally, when the movie let out and everyone chatted while slowly scattering to their cars, Brydan stopped her.

"Let's get some coffee and doughnuts. Know anywhere we could go?" Brydan asked.

Lizzy raised an eyebrow. "How about Krispy Kreme, and then there's a picnic table by a stream Paul and I found last week by the mall. How 'bout it?"

"Sounds good," her friend had answered, sweeping a bow. "After you, Madame'."

Two years later, after maintaining a long-distance relationship on two separate 270-foot cutters on opposite sides of the East coast, they were married.

One year after that, they were still apart. Brydan had completed his last patrol almost two weeks prior. He would report to the Group in Portsmouth next week, and she was technically already out. Her terminal leave had started three days ago, but it was the end of the patrol, so she was stuck for the duration.

"Needs of the Service..."

People often asked why they weren't stationed closer together. The answer was simple: the Coast Guard had a year to move married members. And when they did move Coastie spouses within a 50-mile radius, they could station them wherever they pleased, and at whichever units they pleased.

You weren't issued a Coastie spouse in your seabag, Petty Officer Townsend. Now turn to.

Lizzy and her husband decided not to even tempt the system: she was getting out. She was tired of the macho dick-matching attitude of the boys she worked with. She learned quickly and was hard-working--she could do well anywhere. At least, that's what her supervisors and college professors had always told her throughout the years, even before the Coast Guard.

"But," her first XO had warned her. "Your temper is going to get you in trouble someday. You're too quick to put people on your shit list."

In Portsmouth, of course there were shipmates on the *Buzzard* she didn't get along with, but they were the distant minority—exactly two. She worked her ass off, and as a result she was not only accepted, but liked. All the engineers went to bars together in ports-of-call, and she would slam her shots of tequila and whiskey as she listened to the Firsts and Chiefs swap sea stories. She would go to people's houses on Sundays for football games. She had no idea how good it was--until she went to the *Surveyor*.

There were many factors working against her on the *Surveyor*. 270s inherently seem to have a cloud of gloom hanging over them. The previous year, the *Surveyor* was underway 203 days out of 365, and that was a typical schedule as far as 270s went. Tempers flared, morale was always low, and politics ran rampant as officers raced to collect bullets for their evaluations at the expense of their crew's sanity. Patrols were often expanded, ports shortened or cut, and boredom was a poison that slowly strangled any joy or pleasure on board. Uncertainty was the only thing one could count on.

She also recognized too late that she came on too strong when she first came aboard. She tried too hard to make a good impression, and she pissed off the guys in her shop. On a smaller ship, or perhaps on land, things might have been smoothed over. But, as three other DC guys gelled together and worked as a team, she figured they had decided that she wasn't wanted. As a result, as per unwritten rules, her department didn't accept her, and in turn the entire engineering department didn't, either. She was isolated these past three years, and while there were people in other departments to hang around with, it hurt nonetheless.

Lizzy was suddenly snapped out of her thoughts by the awareness that the sun was almost down.

*Shit,* Lizzy realized. *I have the mids. I should be in the rack. Damn it!*

As she turned to go into the helo hanger, she heard a small intake of breath around the corner, followed by a catch. Curious, Lizzy turned the corner to the starboard side of the helo deck, and peered around to the MSB boat davit.

To her amazement, the Captain was looking over the water, and there were...tears running down his face? He was crying?

*Don't need to be here,* Lizzy quickly thought as she whipped back around the corner and into the helo hanger. She turned around and scanned the flight deck. No one else was there.

*I wonder what that was about?*

Lizzy wasn't going to tell anyone about it, since it probably was a death in the family or something. She might have turned into an absolute bitch living with the assholes, but she still had scruples. None of her business, or anyone else's.

Still curious, but figuring she'd never know the big secret, she went down below to sleep for a few hours.

◆ ◆ ◆ ◆

*Six Hours Later*

"So then we look out over the Fo'c'sle, and SA Humphries was naked, covered in white paint, with this sheet around his shoulders. He had climbed up the Jackstaff, and was flyin'." MK1 Donaldson stared blankly at a point in space as he slowly moved his arms up and down, imitating the crazed Seaman.

It was 0238, and MK1 Donaldson was in rare form. The four-person watch laughed as stories were swapped and smart-ass comments made. They were all sitting in the Engineering Control Center, a sound-insulated booth where the console for the engineering systems was located. It was right next door to the Engine Room. Lizzy and Tomelli made rounds every hour, but came back to ECC to hang out and stand by in case of emergencies. Lizzy was pleased with the watch-- she didn't mind any of the people in that compartment. MK1 was EOW, EM2 Llewellyn was the Throttleman, Lizzy was Auxiliary, and FN Tomelli was Security. Lizzy had a cool but companionable relationship with Tomelli, whom everyone called Tommy, even though his first name was Bill. She and Tommy had conversations when they were on watch together, but even with the nonrates there were limits. She liked all of them, but she could never get totally comfortable. Everyone busted on everyone—and the cruelest cuts came when the person wasn't in the room. She had no idea what they said about her, but sure as shit she was put in their grinder, too.

But, it always pays to be at least outwardly friendly, especially on the 0000-0400 watch, so she asked MK1 what happened to Humphries.

"Helo, next day." MK1 replied, tossing his thumb over his shoulder in an "outta here" motion. "Gone!"

Just then, the phone rang.

"ECC, Petty Officer Donaldson." MK1 paused. "Yeah, she's here." As he listened, he turned and looked at Lizzy with a puzzled look on his face.

27

"OK, I'll tell her." MK1 hung up and gazed at Lizzy, concerned.

Lizzy got nervous. "What is it?"

MK1 glanced at Llewellyn, then back at her. "That was Todd. The Captain sent Phillips to wake up Johnny to relieve your watch. When you're done with that, report to the XO."

Lizzy felt the bottom of her stomach drop down around her hips. "Did they say what was wrong?"

MK1 shook his head. "I can't imagine what they want at this hour. Has anyone been sick in your family?" He grimaced.

Lizzy shook her head no. She didn't feel like talking. Everyone got quiet.

As she sat there, she felt herself go into her bulldog mode. Her muscles tensed, she felt her mind tunnel to a pinpoint. Her eyes narrowed, and her perceptions enhanced. She got like this during underway drills, which made the DCTT team members pull her aside and whisper, "Calm down," like she was about to go ballistic.

Actually, inside Elizabeth was very calm. It was her body preparing itself to resolve whatever crisis was upon her, whether it was a mainspace fire, her father in the hospital again, or some punk-ass nonrate deciding that he didn't need to listen to her. But, she was always in complete in control of herself. She might bowl people down and completely take over, but the job would get done. She found Malcolm X's signature phrase, "By any means necessary" to be her mantra in times like these.

In this case, she figured her father was dying—he had had heart problems for years--and she went through the steps in her mind: *OK, call the Red Cross, send a message to Brydan; see if they'll order a helo; pack one bag for the trip home...*

Johnny walked in ten minutes later, looking sleepy and annoyed but maybe there was a tinge of worry in his eyes for Lizzy, even though they had never gotten along. "OK, whatcha got?"

Lizzy took a breath. "Number one main on-line, number two in five minute standby. Number two generator on-line, one is put to bed. Evap on dump, I just filled number one main's sump a half-hour ago, fins are on, everything else is fine."

"OK, I've got it." Johnny looked at MK1 and nodded.

"Go on," MK1 told her. "Good luck."

Lizzy threw her earphones on and ran into the Engine room. She went down the ladder, rushed along #1 MDE, and raced up the short ladder to the half-deck. Even though the hydraulic door that led to Auxiliary 1 was supposed to be for emergencies only, Lizzy thought this was a good enough reason to use it, rather than going through the trouble of the Engine Room scuttle. She pushed the button and waited impatiently as the door slowly rolled on its wheels. Finally, she pushed through and sprinted up the ladder.

The ladder emptied to a small passageway that led to the main passage. BM2 Phillips was there, coming from the mess deck with a cup of coffee in her hand, on her way to the bridge. She had the BMOW.

"Erin, what the fuck is going on?" Lizzy tried to keep her voice down as they both hurried down the passageway to the topside ladder. All the lights were on red on the main deck, and Lizzy was trying to adjust her eyes to the dimness. The white lights were on 24 hours a day in the engineering spaces.

"The hell if I know," Erin muttered. "The Captain got a message an hour ago, and no one knows what the hell it said, even the Radio watch. When the Captain was woken up, he went down there himself to read the message. Seb had to leave the room." Erin shook her head. "Can't be good. Parsons said the Captain was getting messages all evening like that."

"Anyone else been called in to see the XO?" Lizzy asked as she darted up the ladder, Erin following behind.

"Supply," Erin lowered her voice as they reached the top of the ladder, where the XO's office was. Erin was referring to the Supply Officer, Mr. Goddard, a CWO-3.

Lizzy stood at the door, and then glanced at over her shoulder. "I'll let you know." Erin was Grapevine Central on the pig, and it paid to keep her well stocked with valuable and/or unusual information, in case a person ever needed a favor.

Erin nodded, and then wound her way to the Bridge.

Lizzy noticed white light coming from beneath the XO's office door. She knocked softly.

"Come in," the XO called.

Lizzy pushed the door opened and stepped inside. The sudden change from red light to white light blinded her for a second, but she quickly adjusted.

The XO's office was also his stateroom, so his desk stood in one corner of the compartment, his rack in the other. The XO was a small, thin man, about 35 but already graying along the temples. Lizzy tried to remember the last time she spoke to him--she usually tried to avoid officers. He was sitting at his desk. He wore coveralls and hadn't combed his hair, and was looking grim as she looked for a seat. There was one chair other than the XO's desk chair, but Supply was already in it.

"Go ahead and sit on the rack, Townsend," the XO said softly. "You'll want to be sitting for this one."

Lizzy sat. She hoped the XO would come to the point--Lizzy never liked suspense, even the pleasant kind. And especially not at 0300.

The XO didn't disappoint her. He swiveled his chair so he faced the two of them, and spoke: "Last night, the Captain got a message from Headquarters." The XO paused, but only for a second. "It seems there has been a nationwide epidemic going on this past week. They think it's a virus of some kind, but it makes the victim absolutely mad. Violent. Blood-hungry. The entire east coast Metropolis area is in chaos. We're talking from Portland, Maine to Washington, DC. And this virus is spreading like a wildfire South and West. Millions are dead. We know nothing about it, but the government is taking precautions to keep us safe."

Lizzy felt the blood drain from her face. *My God...all those people... Brydan?*

The XO continued: "We were lucky. We've managed to isolate the military families at Patton." Patton Air Force Base was where most of the families lived. "They are in barracks under guard. The DOD has taken over evacuation of all military personnel. When we return to Newport, we all will be escorted to Patton."

He paused again. He sighed.

"I'm not telling the crew until morning, and after they're told, things are going to get very ugly around here. The reason I called the two of you here is so you got a heads-up about the situation. We're having problems finding your spouses.

The XO turned to Mr. Goddard. "Jim, your wife was visiting relatives in Oakland, according to your neighbors, and National Guard troops have been unable to find her there.

"However," The XO continued, "The virus hasn't reached the West coast in force yet. We are hopeful we can track her down. I wouldn't worry yet." Goddard slumped into his chair, staring into space.

Then the XO turned to Lizzy, and she knew by looking into his eyes that her world was about to crumble. "Elizabeth, your husband went on stand-down with the rest of the crew ten days ago. The outbreak started during their 72's, and he never reported for duty. Over three quarters of the crew is missing. They don't have a lot of hope of finding any of them alive..."

Lizzy didn't hear anymore. Her mind shut out everything else as images of Brydan raced through her head. She felt herself sinking as she remembered his smile, how he felt in her arms, and their plans for the future...

*Brydan? God, please, no...no...not my husband...*

***NO! PLEASE, GOD!***

She was told later that the entire bridge crew went cold at horrible scream that came from the XO's stateroom. Lizzy didn't remember saying anything. She didn't remember the XO, Phillips, and SN Revel carrying her down to the female berthing, she didn't remember being half-thrown in her rack. She didn't remember Doc coming in and injecting her with a sedative so she would stop screaming, so the rest of the females could go back to sleep.

None of them did, though. Instead, they lay in their racks, shivering, wondering what it was that finally forced Townsend over the edge.

# ✦CHAPTER SIX✦

*Newport, RI*
*Ten Days after Infusion*

On a bright sunny day at 1230, the crew of the CGC *Surveyor* saw the waterfront of the Newport Naval Base. Along the pier there were no less than fifty marines, all in fatigues, each one carrying an M-16. The Navy provided the line handlers, which under normal circumstances would have been most unusual, since Pier 2 was officially for the Coast Guard, and unofficially the Navy never bothered to help the Coast Guard with anything. But, there they were, and the mooring went without incident.

Lizzy Townsend was on the 03 Deck, sitting against the white box that held the signal flags, arms wrapped around her knees. She was in her coveralls and boondockers, snuggled in her float coat. She should have been on the flight deck handling fenders, but she didn't feel like it, and no one pushed her.

This was the first time that she hadn't taken drugs on schedule since the XO told her husband was missing. She had begged to Doc two days ago that the injections were making her feel like a pincushion. With some hesitation, Doc finally unlocked his narcotics locker and tossed a bottle of Demerol to her.

"Take one every six hours," Doc had told her. "Do not try to overdose. I'll be sending people randomly to check on you, and if you try to kill yourself, I will personally pump your stomach and make you wish I never gave you these pills. You understand me?"

She promised she would be good. Hell, Doc had chosen her drug wisely. On Demerol, she didn't give a damn about anything--and who would ever want to leave that ride? She had taken her last pill at 0600 that morning, so she still felt very cozy and right with the world. And she still had three pills left...

It is not Standard Operating Procedure in the Coast Guard to keep their personnel drugged up on addictive narcotics for three days. But, these were unusual times and, frankly, no one seemed to give a damn about protocol anymore; what was important was to get everyone to Rhode Island in one piece. Surprisingly, no one had committed suicide or hurt themselves on the *Surveyor*, which was more than some other ships could say. According to message traffic and BM2 Phillips, the *Benson* had a GMC blow a hole through the roof of his mouth with a 9mm only two days ago on route to San Francisco, and a BM3 on the *Courage* was found in the Boatswain's Hole, dangling from three-strand line.

It was amazing that the crew managed to get the ship into Rhode Island at all, even with a full complement. The Captain had shut himself up in his stateroom, leaving the XO to run the ship and counsel the crew. And, on top of everything else, they even managed to have a Charlie fire in aft steering.

The only things that kept the crew going were two important events: e-mail three days before from the families at Patton, assuring their Mommies and Daddies that they were fine; and the news that Supply's wife had been found safe in Oakland. This gave the single crewmembers hope that their parents and loves ones might be OK, too.

Lizzy had missed all of this excitement. Normally, someone flipping out would mean a one-way ticket on a helicopter the next day, just like SA Humphries in

31

MK1 Davidson's story. Now, they kept her under sedation (well, she kept herself under sedation) and she spent the time in her rack, only leaving to use the toilet.

At first she didn't eat or drink, either, but the ship's yeoman, Claire, insisted on bringing meals to her and wouldn't leave her alone until she ate at least half. While she ate, Claire would fill her in on the scuttlebutt.

*Claire is a good friend*, Lizzy now mused, hugging her knees.

Lizzy picked herself up and walked across the deck to look over the starboard rail. No less than ten crewmembers were struggling to get the lifelines down and to get the brow over the side.

*Wow, no one had to beg for people. This is a first...*

Once the brow was over, five Marine officers came aboard and made a beeline to the door leading to Officer Country. Right behind them were three members of the Health Services Corps. One of them approached SN Revel. SN Revel saluted the officer.

"Where's your corpsman?" the Doctor asked.

"Right here," Doc jogged up to the officer and saluted. "HS1 Harris, Sir."

"HS1," the Doctor began, "Where are your Section Eight cases?"

Harris winced. "FA Lee was in his rack an hour ago, SK2 Williams was on the mess deck, and DC2 Townsend was on the 03 deck." Harris nodded up towards the mast.

"Get them together ASAP and meet me on the mess deck. My two companions and I have to do a quick eval to figure out if they'll go with the rest of the crew, or if they have to be hospitalized."

Just then the flight deck's door handle slammed up, the door flew opened, and the five Marine officers burst into the helo hangar.

"WHERE'S HARRIS?" the leader boomed.

Harris paled. "Here, sir!"

The Major stalked towards the Petty Officer. When he spoke, his voice was low.

"When was the last time you saw your Captain?"

"An hour ago, Sir!"

The Major shook his head. "You'd better pray the autopsy agrees with you, corpsman, because we just found your Captain in his Stateroom with his brains blown out."

*An Hour Later*

"Now, DC2 Townsend, lay to the Chief's Mess. Townsend, Chief's Mess."

Lizzy made her way down the main passageway going aft, still a little pissed off at the other DC's. She might have gone nuts, but she still knew how to hook up sewage, the fucking assholes...

She strolled up to the Chief Mess door and knocked.

"Come in."

Lizzy opened the door and peeked inside. There was only one person inside the compartment, a Marine officer—a female who seemed a little chunky for a marine. She had Lieutenant bars.

Lizzy was trying to remember. *That would make her a...*

"I'm Captain Lewis."

*That's right--Lieutenant is the same as Captain.*

"Please come in." She waited for Lizzy to enter and shut the door behind her. "I've been assigned to be a crisis counselor for the Health Services Corps. I have ten minutes to decide if you're stable enough to continue with your crewmates off this base, or if we need to transfer you somewhere else."

Lizzy stared at her. "Ma'am?"

The captain smiled. "It's OK--Your XO briefed me about you. We're just going to go over a few things. Please take a seat, Elizabeth. May I call you that?"

Lizzy sat across from her. "Please call me Lizzy."

Captain Lewis nodded, and then continued, focusing on Lizzy's eyes. "You didn't react violently to the news of the virus. According to your XO, you reacted to the news about your husband. Losing control is a natural response to the sudden loss of a spouse."

Lizzy squeezed her eyes shut. "He hasn't been pronounced dead yet," she said shakily.

Lewis nodded. She reached for Lizzy's hand and grasped it. "That's true. However, I need to know how you're dealing with this--with all this."

Lizzy looked up at Lewis. She choked back a sob and pulled her hand away.

"How do you think I'm doing?" she cried.

*God, Lizzy realized to herself. The Demerol must be wearing off.*

"Sorry, Ma'am." She took a deep breath, and tried to ignore the tears tickling her cheeks.

"We had waited for...for so long to be together..." Lizzy began, but her voice broke. She took another breath to speak again, but she needed to change the subject for a moment.

"Can you..." She swallowed. "Tell me...where the crew is going from here?"

Lewis frowned. "They didn't tell anyone about that?"

Lizzy's mouth twitched in a grimace. "I've...been kinda out of it the past few days."

"In that case...yes," Captain Lewis replied, letting out a breath.

"There are four buses waiting outside the pier. Two buses will take the married members to Patton to be reunited with their families. From there, they'll be transported to safe places in undisclosed locations."

Lizzy nodded. "And the single members?" she whispered.

"That's a little more complicated. The other two buses will transfer them to temporary quarters. A hanger has been outfitted with telephones—a couple hundred of them. You and the remainder of your crew—if you choose to go with them—will have twenty-four hours to track down your families. If you are successful in reaching them, you will be permitted to bring your immediate family along. That means parents and any brothers or sisters you may have. If you can't find them, and if you can find another person, you can take them with you. If you find a friend with a husband, exceptions will be made on the case-by-case basis."

"Excuse me," Lizzy interrupted. "But come along where?"

"Other safe places in other undisclosed locations." Captain Lewis replied with a straight face.

Lizzy nodded again.

Captain Lewis checked her watch. "We're almost out of time, Lizzy. I need to know where you want to go. I'll be honest: I don't think you need to go for a psych board. You're not crazy, you're grieving."

Lewis' mouth stretched into a thin line. "And, to level with you, there

33

really isn't anywhere else for you to go. As soon as the government has packed up all it can, it will probably disappear from here entirely, and whether you survive that or not will depend on which side of the fence we both decide you're on. Right now, the military is the last stronghold modern society has left, and every serviceman is packing up and heading west.

"So, are you going with them, Lizzy?"

Lizzy thought about it for a moment, then looked at Lewis and gave her a grim smile.

"With an invitation like that, how could I refuse?"

◆  ◆  ◆  ◆

The crew was busy packing for the next two hours. The single people had been instructed to pack only one seabag with some civilian clothes thrown in, but it quickly turned into one seabag and whatever else could be carried into the unknown. Many of the females packed pictures, stuffed animals, old love letters, and well-loved novels. All of the single crewmen who had address books or cell phones packed them for the fateful twenty-four hours at the hangar.

Lizzy packed her issued seabag, her photographs, two outfits of civilian clothes, her MP3 and some CDs, stolen AA batteries from the DC shop (enough to last a year, Lizzy figured), some favorite Christina Dodd novels, and her traveling guitar. As she unstrung the instrument, Lizzy wondered if she could get her guitar to wherever they were going without making it kindling. She was going to attempt it; she didn't know where she'd end up, and how bored she would be there. If there was one thing you learned to anticipate after time on a ship, it was boredom...

Of course, the crew was doing more than packing. Friends were saying farewells, and a last meal was hastily fried up to be scarfed down as people could find room on the mess deck. The crew was somber and quiet. They were told buses would be pulling out at 1600--with or without them.

All over the ship, Navy personnel were scurrying about, working to prepare the *Surveyor* for mothballs, a process that would usually take months. Groups were in AMS 1 and 2, flushing the sewage system. Another team pumped fuel from the tanks into trucks on the pier. Yet another packed up all the medical supplies and hand-carried them to a waiting Dodge Caravan. Anything that wasn't bolted down was leaving the ship in trucks and transports. The *Surveyor* crew noticed that they seemed to work by rote, which was a disturbing thought. Talking was kept to a minimum, as if the cutter was already a dead ship.

Finally, without ceremony or circumstance, the crew of the *Surveyor* lumbered down the gangplank and onto the waiting buses. As they boarded, some of the members of the crew suddenly paused.

"Do you hear that?" ET3 Robbins asked aloud to no one in particular.

YN1 Shaw strained to listen. She paled. "Gunshots." she said.

"And shouting," ET3 Robbins added. The procession moved faster.

Lizzy noticed each of the grayish-blue buses had oversized tires and what looked like a cow puncher below their grills, like on the front of locomotives. *That's an odd thing to have on a...*

*...that red isn't rust, is it?*

Then the buzz of an engine in the distance interrupted her thoughts.

Ahead, the crew could see a jeep speeding down the road towards the pier, spewing dust behind it. It flew through the checkpoint and hadn't even stopped before a soldier in the passenger seat stood and began screaming.

"MOVE IT!" he bellowed. "AN INFECTED PACK IS REPORTED IN THE AREA, SO WE JUST RAN OUTTA TIME! Let's-go-Let's-go-LET'S-GO!"

Everyone scrambled on the buses, marines climbing onboard last. Lizzy sat down next to Claire on the front bus as the bus engine roared to life and the driver shifted gears. On her bus, one marine stood at the opened front door, and the other stood at the opened back exit; both were carrying M-16s.

"God, I hate this!" one marine screamed to the other over the roar of the bus' diesel engine.

"At least there's only one more after this!" the other one shouted in reply.

The crew sat two in each seat, too frightened to speak as they bounced around.

The buses sped out down the road, twisting and turning towards the main gate. As they approached, the passengers could see three guards in fatigues swinging open the two wire-mesh barriers that kept the base isolated from the rest of the world. The buses zipped through them, and then the gates were shut behind them. If they could, the crew of the *Surveyor* would have then heard the *click* of the gate locking after them, followed by the *bzzt* of the electric breaker surging 5,000 volts through the fence. It was a jerry-rigged, last-minute instillation, but the electricity worked effectively.

Two seconds later, down about a quarter mile, four corpses lay smoking and twitching on the outside of the fence, surrounded by older charred and decaying bodies. Those Infected hadn't made it.

Two other Infected were on the correct side, hands ripped opened from the razor-sharp barbed wire, running towards the closest buildings.

*We have finally made it. Who can join us?*

◆  ◆  ◆  ◆

*Massachusetts, Near Cape Cod*

The buses had an hour drive before they arrived at Patton. The atmosphere in the bus was tense--no one talked. Some went into a fitful sleep, others watched out the windows.

As they had traveled up I-195 towards Massachusetts, the landscape was something out of a bombing aftermath. Trails of black smoke were silhouetted against the sky, marring the colors of the sunset. When the road passed near a town or city, the passengers could see that usually it wasn't the whole town in flames, but rather random buildings. There were cars in the streets, but no vehicles were moving. No people were in sight.

The quiet was absolutely unnerving. It was 5:30 pm, and normally the interstate would be packed with rush-hour commuters. Now, the highway was completely empty, except for one military transport that passed going the other direction around New Bedford. No one thought they'd ever miss traffic jams, but now they would have given anything to see even one civilian car on the highway: people honking their horns, cutting each other off, giving each other the finger...it would've been downright heartwarming.

Around Bourne, MA on I-195 the landscape opens up to a wide valley to the right of those traveling eastbound. Those that were still awake on the buses and

35

looking out the windows took a collective gasp. They were rewarded for their wakefulness with a sight that made their hearts stop with terror and ran their blood cold.

It was dusk. In the center of the valley, about a mile away, they saw a herd of humans *en masse* making their way across the landscape. There must have been hundreds of them. They appeared to be mostly naked and they moved mindlessly, chaotically, and violently, the sea of Infected rippling with arms and legs as it traveled. The mob left bodies scattered behind it, those that slipped and were trampled within the mass. Lizzy took the entire valley in, and noted houses in its wake were surrounded by flesh-colored blobs. The mob seemed to be traveling parallel to the highway, looking for the next town to descend upon to rip apart and destroy.

Lizzy turned away and pulled opened her knapsack. In the fading light she searched for her bottle of Demerol, hands shaking and eyes wet. Her mind was going into overdrive, and she was imagining Brydan wallowing in a mass of hungry naked animals, being ripped to pieces and trampled on the ground and left to rot. He was screaming in pain as they pulled limbs off his body...

Lizzy felt like she was going to vomit. The image was more than she could take without assistance. Her fingers closed around the bottle, and she pulled it from the depths of the sack in triumph.

Claire, who was sitting beside her, leaned in and whispered, "How many does that make today?"

Lizzy pushed down on the child-resistant cap and twisted. "Two doses."

Claire frowned. "Those are going to be harder to stop taking the longer you use them, you know."

Lizzy opened the bottle and pinched a white pill between her two fingers. "I doubt I'll be able to get more where we're going, so I might as well enjoy them while they last." She popped the pill in her mouth and swallowed.

Claire shook her head and turned away, not saying another word.

The bus driver had a headset with an earpiece in his left ear, and every so often he would press his finger to it, and then press a small button on the microphone above his mouth and mutter a short response. About ten miles from Patton, something changed. He began a conversation in low tones, but sounded urgent. Finally, he looked over his shoulder.

"Newport called Red Blossom. We're going to be staying at Patton."

The two marines nodded to themselves and sadly turned back toward their opened doors.

"Jesus," is all the rear marine said.

The BMC, who was sitting right behind the driver, leaned forward. "What's Red Blossom?"

The driver didn't turn around, but kept his eyes on the road and said grimly, "They've been taken over. We can't go back."

The chief leaned back and silently meditated on this in the dark. Though the sun had gone down, the overhead lights on the bus were left off. The only light came from the headlights and the luminescent glow of the radio panel.

Lizzy also took this in.

*I hope Captain Harris got out*, she thought.

Finally, there was a white glow far in the distance. The marines closed the doors and the one in front turned towards the other passengers. He spoke in a loud, practiced tone, like he had done it several times before.

"All right, listen up. The Infected always hang around outside the base. You may even recognize some people in the mob. What you must know is that this bus cannot stop for ANY reason. We will be shooting people. We will be running over people. But we have to do this to stay alive: you don't know what they're capable of.

"Stay on the bus. If you jump off, we will not rescue you. If I were you, I would sit back, cover your ears, and close your eyes until this is over. I wish I could. Any questions?"

There was silence, and the marine turned back towards the door.

"Are you ready, Frank?" he called over his shoulder.

The other marine sighed. "Sir, yes, sir."

"All right." The front marine cycled his chamber. Both marines reopened their doors.

The glow was getting closer. Suddenly, the rear marine cycled his chamber and yelled.

"INCOMING!!"

Suddenly the sounds of automatic gunfire erupted and bounced off the walls and ceiling of the bus. Shells clinked on the floor. Several people took the marine's advice, but Lizzy felt the Demerol kicking in, so she covered her ears and watched the action impassively, as if she was watching a movie.

Ahead, she could see flattened people squished into the pavement and live ones standing in the middle of the road, dazzled by the headlights. Seconds later, they would disappear from view, and she could feel the *thump-thump-thump* as the Infected hit the cow catcher and fell beneath the oversized tires. The driver was strategically driving, trying to hit the people so that they would bounce off the side of the catcher. He never swerved to avoid anyone, but stayed on the road at full speed.

Meanwhile, the gate was getting closer, and she could see guns flashing as more bodies fell around the slowly opening gate. A man was standing on a cherry picker on the opposite side of the gate, above the fence, leaning over and shaking his fist.

Lizzy squinted through her fuzziness and impassively wondered what the hell the guy was doing. As they got within fifty yards of the gate, she saw the clear liquid droplets from his hand raining down on the mob.

*What's with the water?* she thought. Then she saw the Infected clawing at themselves where the water landed and...was that smoke coming off their skin?

*Wow...is that acid or something?*

By then, the two buses were inside the base, and the gate was slammed shut. The M-16s went silent, and both buses lurched to a halt.

The front marine kicked at the shell casings on the floor, trying to clear a path. The brass had to be several inches thick in some places. Both marines had been almost continuously firing for five minutes, maybe more. A knock sounded on the front door, and he opened it. A Coast Guard Captain climbed aboard, patted the shoulder of the driver, and spoke to the passengers.

"You must be the crew of the *Surveyor*. I'm Captain Terrence of Group Melbourne Point."

At this, everyone saw something flash in his eyes and the corner of his mouth twinge in a half-grimace. He looked down at the floor.

"Well...*was* Group Melbourne Point."

No one was surprised by the past-tense. By now, the entire crew was pretty sure "was" described just about everything anymore. After a beat, Captain Terrance looked back up, took a breath and continued his speech.

"I am now the acting Coast Guard liaison for the Patton Air Force Base. I know you've been through a terrible ordeal, but you are all safe now. For the married personnel, your families are anxious to see you and are waiting about a half mile up the road. We will take you there shortly.

"The rest of you, gather your belongings from the rear bus and go to that white warehouse on the right. Take a seat on one of the chairs, and you will receive further instructions in a few minutes."

Lizzy and the other single people grabbed their gear and hauled down the path. What Lizzy noticed right away was the lack of traffic around them. True, it was 1900, but there were maybe six other people in sight. And no one was walking around that didn't obviously have somewhere to go.

The group filed into the warehouse. It was gutted and barren, with patches of light only where the harsh overhead lights cut through the dim. The warehouse was a large space about seven hundred feet square with an opened ceiling. It was clean and dry, with no sheetrock walls--just the metal skin and joists. The floor was poured concrete, and if one looked close enough, one could clearly see the rust stains where the individual steel storage cages used to be bolted to the floor before the virus. Rusted bolts were scattered across the floor.

The first thing they noticed in the warehouse was the rank and file of desks in the center. There must have been eighty desks or more, all with telephones of different styles and colors. Wires were strewn everywhere.

*They must have come from the housing units*, Lizzy thought.

There were rows of folding chairs arranged half-circle around a podium and a large white dry-erase board. On the board were phone numbers and the words "Have Patience!" written in green block print. The group piled their belongings in a corner and took seats in the semi-circle. A few minutes later, an African-American woman dressed in a maroon business suit passed through a side door and walked to the podium, her high heels clicking on the concrete. She stopped behind the podium, made sure everyone was paying attention, and began to speak.

"My name is Lydia Matthews, and I work for the counseling center here on base. My job is to help those who are single, or those who have lost spouses, to adjust to these changes we are all going though.

"I don't have to tell you, this is a very scary time in our history. Something..." She paused. "Something is infecting the citizens of not just our country, but of the world. We don't know a lot about this plague, but we are learning more and more about it each day. What did your command tell you? What was the last you heard?"

Claire, being the highest ranking single person, raised her hand. "They thought it was a virus, and it had spread all over the east coast, and it made people crazy, and there was no cure."

Lydia nodded. "We know more than that now. I need you all to brace yourselves for a shock."

Everyone tensed up except Lizzy. DC2 Townsend was relaxed in her seat, trying to look interested but not doing a very good job. With the narcotic active in her body, she was confident she could handle any change in physics Lydia wanted to throw at her. Lydia could tell them gravity was about to leave the Earth, and Lizzy would smile and nod and wait to float in air.

"They're demons." Lydia said frankly.

# ·CHAPTER SEVEN·

*Patton Air Force Base*
*Building 12*
*2230*

*Well,* Lizzy thought through her haze. *That's something...*

The rest of the group stared at the counselor, mouths agape.

"I know it's hard to believe." Lydia continued. "We're not sure where they come from, or why they have such power now, but I shall tell you what we do know.

"It started near Albany, New York. They can enter the body through one of two ways that we know of. One is what the church would call possession when the demon, through its own will, takes over the human host. Or, they take over through direct blood-to-blood contact, which is how they have spread so fast. One cut or bite is all they need.

"Multiple demons can infect a single body. Often, they use one body as transportation and then distribute themselves over a wide area. You are already familiar with the results so far.

"Right now, the only way to get rid of the demons is to inflict the body with enough pain that the body goes into shock and the demon loses its hold. This, unfortunately, usually means permanent damage. Or worse."

Lydia paused and looked around the group. "Any questions so far?"

Lizzy raised her hand unsteadily. "What about the guy in the cherry picker? What was he throwing at the people?" Lizzy's voice was loud and a little too succinct, like she was over-pronouncing her words.

Lydia raised her eyebrow, but answered the question.

"He is a Catholic priest. He says that he can use holy water to exorcize the demons in the name of Jesus Christ. The United States government doesn't have much to say about that but, as you saw, the water hurts the Infected enough to delay them." She shrugged. "So, why not? You will all be tested for this skill later, along with some other tests.

"But for now, you all have phone calls to make. Make as many calls as you like. You have twenty-four hours to find your loved ones. Remember: parents, brothers, sisters. Or, one friend. Any other considerations, please see me or my staff. Good luck."

She turned away from the podium and walked around while the group jumped up and swarmed towards the phones. Lizzy remained in her seat, drained of her energy all of a sudden.

The counselor crossed her arms and looked at the bedraggled woman in front of her. The glassy eyes, the unwashed body and hair, the disregard for a proper uniform...there was at least one in every boatload, she thought. Silently, Lydia used her eyes and will to make Lizzy look up and into her eyes. Inexplicably, Lizzy felt the irresistible pull and raised her head. Without saying a word, Lydia ordered Lizzy to come to her. Lizzy got to her feet and met Lydia at the center of the semi-circle.

Lydia gave Lizzy a knowing look. "What's your name?"

"Petty Officer Townsend."

"Umm-hmm. What are you on, Petty Officer Townsend?"

Lizzy fought to clear her head enough to hold an intelligent conversation. "I don't know what you're talking about..."

"Don't try to snow me, please." Lydia interrupted. "I've seen this too many times before. What are you taking?"

Lizzy sighed. *This isn't the time to play games*, she decided.

"Demerol."

"From your corpsman?"

Lizzy nodded.

"OK," Lydia sighed. "You need to dry out. Give me what you have."

Lizzy handed over the bottle.

"Concentrate on finding your family for now. It'll help distract you from any withdrawals you might experience. You need to be clean for the tests later on."

Lizzy nodded, feeling miserable.

◆   ◆   ◆   ◆

*Patton Air Force Base*
*Eleven Days after Infusion*
*0430*

Lizzy had tried all of her family members. None of them had picked up their phones. Some lines were eternally busy, some were not in service, and the rest just rang on, and on, and on...

Worse, as the night wore on and the Demerol left her system, she became more and more depressed. She was constantly weeping as she dialed each number. In the end, there were a couple of people who had family in the Midwest that managed to track down someone, but that was all: it was a miserable, horrible night. Sometimes it was hard to hear the receiver through the cries and the wailing of Lizzy's former crewmembers.

There was one number left she wanted to try. The woman wasn't a blood relation, but she was the closest thing to a sister Lizzy had. She lived in the country, so there was a chance. And, it was a cell phone number, which meant if the tower still worked and she had battery...

Lizzy dialed. After one ring, the line clicked, and then there was static.

"Hello?" a voice hoarsely whispered.

For the first time in days, Lizzy felt relief. Maybe even joy.

"Mare? It's Lizzy."

"Lizzy?" The line crackled and Lizzy heard her friend burst into tears. "Oh, thank God!" Mary sobbed. "I thought I would die alone..."

"Listen," Lizzy broke in. "There isn't much time. Where are you?"

"In the basement of my parent's house. I happened to be visiting when they went to work last Wednesday, and then they never came home. I've been down here ever since. You wouldn't believe what I had to rig up to keep the cell phone on..."

"OK," Lizzy interrupted. "The government is moving me west in a couple of days. I don't know where we're going, but they say it's safe. Do you want to come?"

"Oh, yes! I'm so scared. I hear them in the house, but they haven't found me yet."

40

"I'll have the soldiers come get you. Hang on for a few more hours, OK?"

"All right." Mary sounded hopeful. "Tell them to hurry. I'm running out of water, and it's really beginning to smell down here." Mary giggled nervously.

"I'll see you soon. It'll be fine. Keep low." With that, Lizzy hung up.

Lizzy said a small cold prayer of thanks, out of habit rather than out of true gratefulness to any higher power, and then stood to find a counselor.

She had lost her faith when Brydan had disappeared. She had begun to accept that Brydan was dead. Hope was the knife that twisted in her wounds, and she would rather feel nothing and be done with it. And, above all, dead was far better than, as uncertain as death was, being a part of that twisting, writhing, bloody mob that would haunt her dreams for years to come.

# ·CHAPTER EIGHT·

After a sleepless night of dialing numbers and crying for their loved ones, the single crewmembers of the *Surveyor* were herded to the cafeteria for a quick breakfast, immediately followed by the poking and the prodding of a complete physical and blood work-up. By noon, everyone was grouchy and still a little weepy. After the last of the group was done in the examination rooms, Lydia ushered them to a small waiting area by the clinic's laboratory.

Down the hallway from the waiting area was a set of white double doors, with signs strictly forbidding anyone to enter without authorization. There was a combination lock on the doors, and two armed marines stood in front of them. Lizzy casually looked at the guards, and then leaned against the wall of the sterile white hallway and eased down onto the tile floor about fifty feet from the doors. She was still a little sore from the physical, and now her stomach was starting to churn. She thought the eggs at breakfast tasted funny--she wished she hadn't finished them.

Once everyone had settled in a seat or on the floor, Lydia stood in front of the marines and addressed the group.

"All right, these are the last two tests. After everyone completes these tests, you all can go back to the barracks for some sleep."

She paused as a buzzer sounded behind her. The marines took one precise sidestep away from each other as one of the doors opened and a slightly rumpled young man in a lab coat slipped through. He might have been considered handsome if not for the black rings under his eyes and his pale complexion—he looked like he hadn't slept in days. He nodded to Lydia and smiled slightly. Lydia grinned at him and turned back to the crowd.

"This is Will. He'll be helping you with your tests. Will?" she asked, turning to him again.

"Thank you," he replied, looking around the waiting area. "The first test is simple: there will be a basin of water in the center of the room. We want to see if any of you can make holy water."

The crewmembers stopped looking at him and started looking at each other.

"I know," Will said, "it sounds nuts. However, some people have been able to do it. I can't offer any advice *how* to do it, 'cause we aren't sure ourselves. Howevaa... excuse me," he said as he yawned. "However, we ask you to try."

Lizzy looked down at the floor in front of her. *No fuckin' way...*

Will continued. "I can't tell you what the second test is but, if you can do it, it will become clear very quickly. That's all I can say. Any questions?"

The group looked at him blankly. Will shuffled a little.

"All right," he announced. "Who's first?"

Before anyone could move, Lizzy uncurled herself and went to Will's side. She was feeling worse by the minute, and she wanted to get this over with so she could ask for an antacid. Maybe she could avoid throwing up.

"What's your name?" Will asked.

"Elizabeth Townsend," she replied, swallowing.

Will nodded. He led the way through the double doors and into a large white room. Each wall had a closed door. In the center of the room was a table with the basin of water.

Lizzy felt a wash of nausea sweep over her. She followed Will to the table.

Will gestured to the basin. "OK, give it a shot."

Lizzy shook her head. She was focusing on not salivating—and was failing. Something here was causing her to be sick, and it felt like it was coming from the left door…

"C'mon, Elizabeth, you have to at least try."

Lizzy looked behind her. "What's behind that door?"

Will looked at her blankly. "Why don't you look and find out?" he replied softly.

Lizzy couldn't explain why, but she didn't want to. She started to step forward, but sickness and pain finally overwhelmed her and she fell to the floor, knocking over the basin and vomiting as she fell. Water and puke went everywhere. She curled into a fetal position on the floor, shaking. Her vision blurred, and her head pounded.

"What's happening to me?" she croaked.

Will bent down and began to unfold Lizzy. He sat her up and pulled a handkerchief from his pocket. He wiped her mouth, and then took her hands in his.

"Elizabeth," he said, making eye contact. "We have to go to that door and open it. I can't tell you what's behind it, but if it's what making you sick, this could be very good for you. Will you try for me?"

Lizzy nodded—she was too sick and weak to protest. She managed to get to her feet and leaned against Will as she staggered to the door. With each step the pain in her head got worse, and her arm and leg muscles began to spasm. They reached the door, and Will swung it opened.

Through a haze of tears and intense pain, Lizzy saw three figures sitting in chairs. They seemed to be slumped over.

Will leaned down so his mouth was next to her ear. "Which one?" he asked. "Which one is causing the pain?"

She could barely breathe. The room was fading to black, but she heard herself say, "The right one."

Retching, Lizzy slumped into unconsciousness.

Will quietly gathered Lizzy to his side and clumsily carried her to the far door. Holding her up with one arm, he turned the doorknob with the other and pushed the door opened. Inside was a dimly lit room with four empty beds. Will lowered her to the closest bed on her side so she didn't aspirate her vomit, then turned and left the room. He looked at a plate mirror above the door.

"Our strongest one yet, I think," Will said to the air and giving the thumbs-up sign.

"I think so, too," a voice replied through a speaker in the ceiling. "We may have to make up a category above Level 1 just for her. We'll know with more tests. We'll call some orderlies to clean up the mess, Will. Why don't you take a break?"

"Thank you. I won't be long." Will exited through the main doors and made a beeline to the pharmacy.

William Goldberg had been classified as a Level 3 Sensor, rather average on the Sensor scale, but he also had the unique ability to sense when demon-Infected were awake rather than asleep, which was why he was tapped for this job. All the subjects were sedated in the chair room, including the clean subjects, for their safety as well as the safety of the subjects. If Will sensed the demon-Infected was coming around, the tests had to stop immediately so more anesthesia could be administered. Unfortunately, being around Infected left him with a huge headache.

At the pharmacist's counter, he asked for his usual 1200 mg of Ibuprofen. Palming the tablets, he walked to the water fountain, took the pills, and then sat down to wait for them to take effect. As he sat, he thought about Elizabeth Townsend.

Most people couldn't sense demons or make holy water. Of those who *could* sense demons, maybe one in 1000 could tell which of the three subjects had the demon. And no one that Will had ever seen had reacted like *that*.

Will knew all about what awaited her: more tests, different tests, and more pain.

*At least they'll let her live,* Will thought, *but what a price...*


*1215*


*What the hell's going on?* Anna thought, watching the room beneath her.

Two weeks ago, Anna Martinez was a seminary student at the University of Pittsburgh. Then one day classes were suspended, and Anna ran for her life to the sanctuary of her then-boyfriend's Army base. Chad died the day after she arrived while he was on guard duty. That night, she volunteered to travel to Newport, Rhode Island for Chaplain school. They had been sent to Patton two days ago for additional training. They were told yesterday evening they were staying there until further notice.

That particular morning at Patton, her class was sent to Building 7 at 0900 to observe the tests of the newly indoctrinated. Her class filed into a dark theater in front of a large picture window. Three doctors were already watching two younger men. One of the doctors turned to address the class.

"The tests for the morning are already in progress. Please sit and be quiet. The other doctors and I will explain the procedures later."

Anna was already familiar with the tests: she had failed. She couldn't feel anything or do anything when she was in that same room. She had not noticed at the time, however, was that there was a window near the ceiling.

It was a boring morning until around noon. The lab assistants changed, and after preparing the room Will Goldberg came back with the first of the Coast Guard *Surveyor* crew.

This female looked like she hadn't showered in a week. She was cranky and uncooperative. Then, a few seconds later, she was on the floor, vomiting. The first doctor, who seemed to be in charge, turned toward the other two doctors.

"Did you see that?" he asked them, excited.

"Who is it?" the second doctor asked.

The third doctor leafed through a stack of folders on a desk and pulled one from the pile. "Elizabeth Townsend, a DC2."

"Was she sick before?" the second asked.

The first doctor checked the chart in his hand. "No, a clean bill." He looked through the glass at the now-prone female with shining eyes. "Maybe we've found one."

The third one added, "A strong one, too."

The second peered at the window. "Did she just pass out?"

The entire group stared at the scene below.

"Will's carrying her to the chair room."

The group was riveted to the window. After the door was opened, there was a pause, and then the woman went limp.

Will carried her to another room and went inside. When he came out, he turned towards the window, said something, and gave a thumbs-up.

The doctor picked up a phone hanging on the wall and conversed with the young man in quick, quiet tones. Then, hanging up, he turned to the students.

"You're lucky," he said. "That one has been the strongest yet. Some get nauseous, but we have never had that strong a reaction." He looked at the group and finally rested his eyes on Anna. She was the only female in the room. "Have you been tested?"

Anna nodded. "I don't feel anything. Double negative."

The doctor nodded. "The assistant had to leave for a few minutes. Would you go down the stairway there," he pointed, "and you'll find the room the subject is recovering in. Please make sure she doesn't aspirate. Mr. Goldberg should be back soon."

Anna nodded again and started down the stairs. Behind her, she could hear the doctor say, "This is something as Chaplains and Laypersons you may have to deal with…"

She found the door at the bottom of the stairs. She opened it carefully and peered in.

The room was dark, only illuminated by the light of the stairwell and the light of the main room. On one of the beds she saw a large lump.

She slipped in and went to the still figure. The lump of a woman on the bed seemed to be breathing OK, though her breath stank of vomit and bad hygiene. She was on her side, and seemed to be sleeping. Anna turned and started for the door.

"Can I have some water?" she heard a voice mumble from the lump.

Anna answered, "Sure." She turned around and rummaged near the sink in the dark for a cup.

"I have to turn the lights on," Anna finally said. "Watch your eyes." She found the switch and flipped it down.

Bright light flooded the room. The blue lump groaned. "God, I want to die."

Anna turned on the tap and filled a paper cup with water. "I watched you through the window above this room. Guess you've got some strong powers."

The woman chuckled, and then moaned. She sat up slowly. "You want 'em?"

Anna walked back and handed her the cup. "No, though you must have incredible faith!"

The woman took a sip and eyed Anna. "No," she replied. "If there is a God, He doesn't give a shit." Then she looked past Anna at the wall, as if she just remembered something. Tears started to well in her eyes and crawl down her face.

"Hey," Anna said, sitting next to the woman on the bed, "You OK?"

The woman shook her head. "I found out my husband disappeared a few days ago." She choked out a sob. "I miss him."

Anna nodded. "I lost my boyfriend a couple of weeks ago. He was on a tower when the Demon spawn overtook it. He fell off and died." Anna smiled sadly. "We had just started dating, so I really hadn't had a chance to love him yet, but I liked him." Anna leaned over and rested her elbows on her thighs, hands

45

folded. She looked down at the floor. "He saved my life, though. I'm grateful to him. Maybe it was all part of God's plan."

The woman snorted. She sipped again from the cup.

The Chaplain student decided it was time to change the subject. "My name's Anna." She held out her hand.

The woman took it and grasped it firmly, like a man would. "Call me Lizzy." She released the handshake. "So," she said with a sigh, "what happens now?"

Anna shrugged. "No idea. I didn't get this far in the testing. All I know is, most folks stay about a week, and then they get shipped out west somewhere. I'll be leaving after my school. Did you find anyone to go with you?"

Lizzy nodded. "An old high school friend."

Anna smiled. "That's good. They managed to find my nephew, Joe, in Chicago. Poor little guy." Anna shook her head and tried to fight back the tears and nausea she experienced whenever she thought of him. "He had to hide under his dead mamma to escape the Infected. Poor Vanessa. She would have liked that she saved him, though."

Just then someone knocked on the stairwell door. In the doorway was a male orderly. "You OK, Petty Officer Townsend?"

"Yeah, sure," she said.

"In that case, could you come with me, please? I'm supposed to get you cleaned up. We'll go through the stairwell."

Lizzy stood and wobbled a little as she looked down at Anna. "Good luck."

"You, too," Anna replied. "If you need to talk…"

"You bet," Lizzy said. She followed the orderly out of the room.

Behind her, Anna said a small prayer: for her, for Chad, for Lizzy, and for Lizzy's husband, wherever he was now.

But then the quiet consumed her, and all at once she never felt so alone.

# ·CHAPTER NINE·

*US Miltary Outpost--Female Commune Ruth*
*Somewhere in a Desert*
*Five Years after Infusion*
*0230*

Lizzy had never been sure why there was a night watch.  Even with a full moon, no one could ever see a damn thing.  On this particular night, there was no moon at all, and while the stars shone enough light that the rocks and mountains were slightly lighter than the sky, a batallion could be over the ridge and Lizzy wouldn't notice.  It was a cold desert night—as usual.  Nothing around but sand, cactus, and tumbleweeds—as usual.

And Lizzy had the damn midwatch—as usual.

They were outside the gate, sitting on chairs under a canvas canopy, equipment and food strewn around them.  When the commune was first established, this solitary posting dubbed "the canary watch" would send watchstanders into shaking fits with blatent refusals, even with armed with tasers and shotguns.  Even after five years with no incidents it still made people nervous, but there were enough Sensors to babysit each shift in a 1-in-5 rotation.

*C'mon, you sons of bitches, you wanna live forever?!*

Sara was slumped next to her, head on knees, her body leaning against Lizzy's shoulder.  Every so often, a delicate snore could be heard.  They were both supposed to be awake, but Erin stopped checking about two years ago.  As long as one of the watchstanders was awake and answered the radio she didn't nit-pick.

There was a hiss of static over the commco, and Danielle's sleepy voice crackled after.

"Hey, Lizzy, you there?  Over."

Saying the word "over" sometimes was the only radio etiquette that managed to survive the hacks of Commune Ruth.  Lizzy carefully unclipped her radio from her belt, being careful not to wake Sara.  "Yup, Townsend here.  How ya doin', Danielle?  Over."

"No commune calls, no one loves us."

Lizzy smirked.  Always the same joke...

"Damn the luck.  What's going on?"

"The lab called.  Some breaker went bad.  They need you to come out in the morning."

Lizzy growled deep in her throat.  *God, not again...*

"They'll have to fuckin' wait until 1000.  I'm getting my sleep today."

"It's a breaker for the lab lights.  They want you at first light."

*What the fuck...10,000 PhDs, and not one can change a fuckin' lightbulb...*

"All right," Lizzy's voice was hard over the radio.  "Call the assholes back and tell them I'll be there.  Maybe I can scam a nap from Erin later."

Another voice came over the radio.  "Townsend, this is Olin.  Watch your language and stop whining.  At least you get to leave.  Over."

Lizzy grimaced and her gut tightened.  *Great.*  She nudged Sara awake with her elbow.  "Olin, Townsend.  Roger that.  Over."  Lizzy said through a clenched smile.  Sara sat up and squinted at Lizzy.  *Olin*, Lizzy mouthed silently.  Sara rolled her eyes and rubbed them.

"Townsend, Olin.  Have you forgotten your etiquette?  Over."

*Breathe, Lizzy, don't start, the bitch is just busting balls...*

"Olin, Townsend," Lizzy stated into the commco. "Nope. Over."

Lizzy could swear that she could hear Olin smile over the radio. "Townsend, Olin. So you are going out after muster, right? Over." Olin asked.

"Olin, Townsend. Of course. Over." Cynthia Olin was the XPO, which meant she was second in command and within her rights to make Lizzy get up. Lizzy was of equal rank and could complain to the ONIC, but she didn't want to argue over this.

"Good to hear it. Take Joe with you, and report to me when you're back. Over."

"Olin, Townsend. Roger that. Townsend out."

Lizzy dropped the commco into her knapsack and consciously unclenched her fists.

"What a bitch," Sara said.

"Yeah," Lizzy replied. She looked over her shoulder at Sara. "She won't come out, though. You can go back to sleep."

Sara nodded and dragged herself to her feet. "I'll be back."

"OK." Lizzy stood and stretched. She felt the elastic at the bottom of her jacket rub up her stomach and back as she raised her arms above her head. She dropped her hands and pulled her jacket back down over her hips. Turning away from Sara and her business, she looked into the night.

Erin Phillips, Cynthia Olin, and Lizzy Townsend were all from the *Surveyor*. Lizzy and Phillips were amicable, as friendly as an OINC and her EPO could be. Olin was named XPO only after Lizzy declined the position first. Olin had hated Lizzy five years ago, and probably hated Lizzy even more now.

When BM2/5 Olin was on the ship, she was the queen of the bridge, the darling of the officers, and thought herself the boarding team dynamo. Lizzy was never on the bridge, so interactions were limited. When they were in the same room, they were careful to avoid each other, as if they knew they wouldn't get along.

Lizzy didn't know what started this deep-seated hatred, but Lizzy knew what Olin's malfunction was at the outpost. While Olin was the second-in-command at the Commune, it was little more than a title, since Phillips was a competent OINC and wouldn't let Olin do much. Lizzy, on the other hand, was not only the Primary Sensor for the compound, but was also the EPO and the only DC/ Maintenance Mechanic, which had more unofficial power than Cynthia's official power.

Being the DC, Lizzy was in charge of facilities at the compound, and was on call at the local laboratory about ten miles north of Ruth's current location. With her abilties as a Maximum Sensor, she was sometimes called to the local command headquarters thirty miles SSE from Ruth's current location for confirmations and tests.

Everyone knew Lizzy. Everyone got along with Lizzy--except Olin and her bestest buddy, SK1/6 McMaster. Olin, to her added displeasure and confusion, had friends in the compound but was not as well-liked overall. In addition to being a shrew, Olin thought of herself as the last bastion of military bearing and procedure. This didn't go over well in a mixture of civilians and barely-military females.

Lizzy, on the other hand, made sure your refrigerator kept working.

Sara came back from the rock. "Wake me if there's anything?" She sat back down in the chair.

"You bet," Lizzy replied.

*If there is ever anything...*

*0445*

Lizzy passed the watch to Jackie and Jen and walked with Sara back to the main gate. She looked up.

"DC2/7 Townsend, SN/5 Lane to come in!" Lizzy called to the watchtower.

"Welcome back!" The watch called back. "Muster at 0800!"

Lizzy heard the *click* of the electricial breaker being shut off, and the *creak-creak-creak* of the wheels pulling the chain link gate back.

"Remind me to oil that, Sara," Lizzy muttered out of the corner of her mouth.

"OK," Sara replied.

Lizzy and Sara walked through the gate and into the commune. The commune looked similar to the M.A.S.H. units of the Korean and Vietnam wars. Drab olive green tents littered the landscape. The mess tent was in the center of the compound. The galley was located next door, with collapsable ovens and large propane tanks. The ONIC tent was located on the far side of the commune, the farthest tent from the gate. Fifty sleeping tents were to the north of the mess tent, Workshops and offices were located to the south. A huge childcare center sat next to the clinic. Whenever they had to move, care was taken that the layout of the camp was exactly the same.

Lizzy ducked into her tent. Her tentmate was still sleeping, but when Lizzy turned on her flashlight to rummage through her footlocker, Deana twisted and groaned in her sleep.

"Go back to sleep, Dean," Lizzy whispered. "It's an hour to revellie."

"*Grrummmm.* I hate bein' your roomate." Deana turned over on her side.

"At least I never get pregnant and puke."

"Fuff uff," Deana mumbled from underneath her blanket.

Lizzy found her towel and threw it on her shoulder. She rummaged some more and found her spit kit and shower shoes. Grabbing her coveralls from a peg on the side of the tent, Lizzy wound her way between the dawn-lightened blocks of canvas to the shower houses.

To Lizzy's surprise, water was running, and Erin's stuff was already hanging inside.

"Hey, Erin," Lizzy called. "You in here?"

"Hey, yeah!" BM2/7 Erin Phillips called from the center stall. "Is that you, Liz? I thought you had the mids."

"The lab called," Lizzy replied while she unpacked and arranged her stuff. "A breaker blew, I have to go in."

"WHAT?" The curtain parted and Erin stuck her half-soaped head out. "What kind of bullshit is that? Can't they wait for your wake-up?"

"It has to do with the lights," Lizzy answered as she shrugged out of her jacket. "And, Olin said to go this morning."

"Oh." Erin ducked back into the shower, and the curtain closed. Erin got along with her XPO, so it would take a really special--or really stupid--occasion to override Olin's decisions. Even Erin had to choose her battles sometimes.

"When you get back, take the rest of the day off," Erin added from her shower.

Even though Lizzy wouldn't get back until after quitting time, she appreciated the thought. "Thanks, Erin."

"No problem. Hey, do you think you could take the movies and the books with you? We're way overdue for an exchange. I'm fuckin' sick of watching 'Something about Mary.'"

"OK." Lizzy finished undressing and turned on the shower. Cold water slammed into her arm; she yelped and jumped back with a start. After a few moments, the water warmed up, and Lizzy stepped in.

"Why are you up so early, Erin?"

"Couldn't sleep," Erin replied. "Steph and Polly were having a lover's quarrel this morning."

Lizzy grunted an acknowledging response. There were no men on the compound, and some of the women were either naturally attracted to other women, they were curious, or they were bored. While the US military's policies on homosexuality and fraternization hadn't changed since Infusion, Erin tended to look the other way.

"So why didn't you tell them to shut the fuck up?"

"Ah, I was done sleeping anyway." Erin shut her water off, and Lizzy heard her using her towel. "I'll bring them into my office today. They need to keep their business to themselves, y'know?"

"Yup."

"See you later, Liz." Lizzy heard Erin's footsteps walking out the door.

Lizzy finished her shower and went to the mess tent. This morning called for coffee--lots of coffee. Two laughing toddlers ran into her legs as she walked into the door, almost knocking her down. Once she regained her balance, she saw Joe eating breakfast. She put her cover on an empty peg and walked over.

"Hi, Joe." Lizzy brushed her hand against the young man's shoulder. He was only nine when he was found five years ago, and was too young to go to a man's commune by himself. The Goverment Placement Center decided to place him at Ruth until he turned sixteen. Lizzy figured he felt a little isolated living with a bunch of women and young children, but these trips to the lab were positive distractions. She was trying to get him a job there, so he had less chance of becoming some Navy fag's girlfriend at some Commune David-or-another somewhere.

During a conference at HQ last year, Erin had snuck into a closed-door meeting where the morale issues of male communes were being discussed; what she heard horrified her. When the speaker spoke brightly of the downward trend of reported gang rapes in the communes, Erin left the meeting and began making plans to keep Joe safe. Both she and Lizzy decided getting him hired at the laboratory was the best bet. Joe knew nothing about this, but he was a street-smart kid. Lizzy knew he would figure it out one of these days...

"Hi, Lizzy," Joe said through his eggs. "Goin' to the lab today?"

"Yeah, want to come?"

"Sure." He shovelled more eggs into his mouth. "When are you leaving?"

"After muster. Can you grab the return books and movies from the morale tent?"

"Yeah. I'll tell Anna, and I'll meet you at the truck."

"All right. Remember how to replace breakers?"

"Yup."

"And what wiring's what?"

Pause. "No. I'll bring my book."

Lizzy nodded and went to the coffee urn.  When Commune Ruth began and Lizzy became a DC/MM, the first camp was set up by civilian government workers, with Lizzy assisting.  Those first days went by quickly, blessedly relieving Lizzy of too much free time to mourn and mope for Brydan.  In those eight weeks, the civilians made sure she knew how to assemble the tents, piece together plumbing, jerryrig almost anything with almost anything, and gave her a crash course in electrical systems.  When they left, they issued her a series of old Time/ Life Home Improvement books and some technical manuals in case Lizzy needed instructions about something new.  Joe was borrowing the books at the moment.

Lizzy poured the black liquid that passed as coffee into a plastic mug.  The government supply trucks came on a schedule to drop off food, supplies, parts, and fuel.  She had never had a problem ordering parts, and food was always fresh and plentiful.  Lizzy had no idea where it all came from.  As far as she knew, no one at the commune knew.  The first thing the females were told when they arrived at Ruth was Rule of Survival: All knowledge is on the need to know basis, and *don't ask.*

Because the demons could read the minds of the Infected.  And the last of humanity could end up destroyed.

That golden rule subtly dominated everything at the commune.  It was in the midst of the women's laughing, their talking, and their living.  It kept irritating their sense of peace.  Even the brightest of occasions had those small shadows dwelling in corners.  They could try to convince themselves they were safe at their isolated outpost, but there was so much that they just *didn't* know.  Things their lives depended on.  Like, who knew when the supply trucks would stop coming, and what would happen then?

All the women knew there was a laboratory nearby, but not where it was.  Only Lizzy and Erin knew there was also a local headquarters, and Lizzy knew where both were in reference to their current location.  She had no idea, however, where they were geographically speaking.  Lizzy had seen a map once on Erin's desk with three circles: one was labeled "Ruth," the second "Job," and the third "Joshua."  From this, Lizzy concluded Erin not only could find Ruth on a map, but knew where other communes were in a hundred mile radius or so.

Except for Joshua.  A year after Lizzy saw the map, she was in the radio room when Joshua radioed "Red Blossom."  This was the universal code phrase for demon infiltration, and Ruth bugged out to another location.

It was in the event of a Red Blossom at Ruth that Erin had something else Lizzy had seen only once: a Glock 9mm.  Five years ago Erin had shown Lizzy the full clip of hollow-point bullets.  One of those bullets was for Erin.  Another was for Lizzy.  If Erin couldn't get to the pistol, Lizzy had instructions to kill them both and as many Infected as possible.  It had shaken Lizzy up at first, but now she hardly thought about it.

Over the PA, first call was piped for muster.  Lizzy swallowed the last of her coffee and set her mug in the dishbin.  She grabbed her cover and jogged out the door and into the courtyard.

The only people excused from muster were those on gate watch.  Everyone else was expected to attend.  Those who were on the midwatch, the infirmed--everyone.  A second muster was held at the childcare center.

They stood/sat/laid in formation.  They always lined up in the same rank and the same file.  At 0800 sharp, Erin and Cynthia walked out of the mess tent and stood in front of the assembly.  Each morning began the exact same way:

"Look to your left!"

"Look to your right!"

"Who is missing?"

Those who noticed a person missing would raise their hand, and the discrepancies would be noted. This list would be compared to the watch list. Maybe once a year, a female would come up missing.

It was a sad day when that happened. Outside the military facilities, there was nothing but dead wilderness and demon hordes. Everyone knew that. More importantly, no one who went missing was ever heard from again. Everyone knew that, too.

After roll call, announcements were made by Olin. On this particular day, it was passed that fertility shots were to be given at 1000 for those with last names beginning with A-K.

To herself, for the thousandth time, Lizzy thanked the stars she was not expected to have children. Being a Command Petty Officer, she had the option of having kids or not, and she didn't have time to get pregnant or watch over kids. Rank had its privileges...

Maintenence work requests were getting sloppy, Olin continued, please be more careful, or DC2 Townsend might unplug your range instead of unplug your drain.

Some women politely laughed.

The movies were going to be exchanged today, so tonight's movies will be announced at evening chow. Anyone having children who need shots please see HS2 Jenner.

ONIC needed the order forms for the Uniform Distribution Center by that Wednesday, or people would have to wait until next month.

Any questions, comments, complaints? That was all.

Everyone, military and civilian alike, had jobs to do. The military personnel usually did more of the maintenence, administrative, and guarding duties. Civilians usually handled the childcare and housekeeping responsibilities. Under Erin's command, in any twenty-four hour period all adults were expected to work eight hours, sleep eight hours, and relax for eight hours. Three meals were provided each day, with something sweet for coffee break at 1030. Snacks were given to the children at 1000 and at 1430. Everything and everyone had a time and place and, considering all the circumstances, life at Commune Ruth was pretty good. Lizzy, at least, had no complaints, which is why she never understood why anyone would want to leave. Especially when life on the outside was so...unpredictable.

For her, ignorance was comfortable and blissful. She could live with ignorance. She had seen too much reality for her liking.

Lizzy stopped in the workshop. She had five military females of assorted rates and paygrades, but each had "Maintenence Mechanic" attached to their designators now. In the past, she always had difficulty with the ram-rod enforcement of her will neccessary in almost every supervisor/worker relationship. The threat of expulsion to the Wilderness took care of that problem--her workers were indifferent to her at best, but the work got done, and always on time.

Lizzy opened the screen door to the facilities tent and walked in. The four MM's were sitting around on stools, leaning on butcher block tables. Sara had gone back to sleep after muster.

Jen was in the middle of a story: "So Amy runs in, and we tried to warn her, but she stepped right in the gelatin, slipped, and fell right on her butt—*Boom!* She was *covered* in green goo!"

The women giggled. Lizzy knew they were talking about two toddlers, but except for the slapstick quality of the story she wasn't sure what was so funny.

*Must be mommy humor...*

After the laughter died, the women looked at Lizzy.

"Hi," Lizzy smiled at them. The females muttered various greetings. "Ann, any work orders today?"

A tall lanky marine russeled through papers on her bench. "The XPO said sand is still getting underneath her door."

The corner of Lizzy's mouth twitched. She fought rolling her eyes and closed them instead. "All right, easy fix. Sam, do you think you can get that?"

"Yeah," Sam replied.

"Anything else, Ann?"

More russeling. "The second range is broken in the mess tent. Probably needs cleaning."

Lizzy turned to a sailor. "Tamisha?"

"Got it."

"Is that it?"

The russeling stopped. "Yes."

"OK, I have to go to the lab today--probably an all-day event. Ann and Jen, would you oil the gate wheels? Tamisha and Sam, after your work orders Number Four and Number Eight generators need their monthly PMS. After that, everyone can disappear somewhere."

The women nodded.

"All right. Have fun."

As the girls got off their stools, Lizzy walked past them into the storeroom.

She found the correct cabinet, the correct drawer, the correct bin, and extracted a new breaker. She grabbed her electrical kit bag on the way out to the armory. Once there, she checked out a 22-gauge shotgun and a boxful of shells, and then headed for the truck.

Joe was already waiting in the cab. He glanced at Lizzy as she put her bag in the bed of the truck and then turned back around.

Lizzy opened the driver's door and climbed in. "Pack a lunch?"

"Nope. Miss Bea always feeds me cookies."

"Great. Very nutritious. Anna would freak."

"Anna will never know."

*Good point.* Lizzy started the truck.

Joe was a special case. He wore a blindfold to and from the lab so he didn't know where it was, but he knew everyone in the facility and what they did there. When Lizzy approached Erin about possible security concerns, Erin shrugged.

"If Dr. Maddox is all right with it, it's OK with me," she answered.

Since Dr. Maddox always greeted Joe with a noogie and a "How ya doin', Joe?" Lizzy concluded there wasn't a problem.

Joe put his blindfold on. Lizzy fished through some cassette tapes on the floor and plugged one in the tape deck.

Voices screamed, "*NO!*"

Drums pounded. Guitars blasted.

Joe groaned. "God, not this white-boy shit again..."

"Ah," Lizzy teased, grinning. "You just don't know what's good." She turned it up. The tiny speaker crackled and sounded tinny, but the base was solid.

"*NO SLEEP 'TIL...*" More guitars.

"*BROOKLYN!*"

Lizzy's favorite band, the Beastie Boys, were loud and blaring sound into the truck. And, even better, they were playing her favorite song. Lizzy serenaded Joe at the top of her lungs and danced in her seat while Joe scrunched down into his

53

seat, trying to block out the noise.

When the song was over, Lizzy popped the tape out. "All right, I've had my fix. What do you want?"

"Check the radio first."

It was a tradition Lizzy had given up arguing about a long time ago. She turned down the radio and turned the "tune" dial all the way to the left, then all the way to the right. Nothing but static.

*Hey, the kid might be right sometime,* she thought.

"Nope."

Joe nodded. "OK, get Snoop."

Lizzy got the right tape and popped it in. She turned the volume back up-- it was only fair.

After a few minutes they reached the edge of a deserted town. It had been stripped and cleared of identity long ago--even the street signs were gone. The rare visitor had to follow crumbling landmarks to find the lab.

Left at the Sunoco. Right at the Mom and Pop. Try to ignore the tiny skeleton lying on the sidewalk behind the trash can next to a baby doll. Drive to the end.

Unlike the commune, the laboratory was housed in a permanent stone building that was probably a warehouse. The government kept the outside brick shell and totally refitted the inside.

What was perhaps once the town's eyesore was now its jewel. All the windows were intact. The outside of the brickface was freshly scrubbed. There was even colored stones and cactii out front, carefully landscaped.

The lab was self-contained: all the workers, from Dr. Maddox to the assistant janitor, had berthing. There were volleyball and tennis courts out in the back. Inside, the lab offered recreation rooms, a gymnasium, even an indoor pool. It was luxury living compared to the outpost but, then again, their work was much more stressful. All the females of Ruth had to do was breed.

Lizzy parked along the gate, allowing Joe plenty of room to get out. She grabbed her bag; he grabbed the movie box. They approached the gate.

"Larry!" Lizzy called.

"Hi, Lizzy!" Larry Stratinski was the elderly, eternal gate guard. He hadn't missed a day's work since the lab began. "And Joe's with you! How's the outpost?"

"Dusty." Lizzy and Joe were next to the gate. "Can we come in?"

"Yup. Let me see your signature."

Lizzy pulled her little green notebook out of her back pants pocket and her pen from her shirt pocket. She flipped to a blank page and scribbled her name. She held it up for Larry to see.

"Yup," Larry said. "They can't do that. Come on in."

She heard a *click* and saw the green light go on in the guard shack.

Larry waddled out with a ring of keys and unlocked the padlock on the gate. Lizzy wondered sometimes why the government decided to keep Larry and give him a guard job. The military was never known for its mercy and Larry, she thought, would have been too old for the government to save. There had to be more to Larry than met the eye, but Lizzy figured she would never find out.

"Thanks, Larry," Lizzy said they walked through.

"You're welcome," Larry replied. "Be good, now."

Joe and Lizzy walked through the opening and up the sidewalk to the entrance. Glass sliding doors whisked opened as they approached; it was obvious they were not part of the original building.

The laboratory's interior was primarily white with lime green countertops. The sterility, however, was softened by colorful pictures on the walls and the multi-colored scrubs and lab coats the staff wore. (Except for Dr. Goddard--she always wore crisp white lab coats. It was a powerful statement, though, in the midst of the textured chaos of colors.) The lighting in the labrooms was warm and easy on the eye.

Well, except in Lab 1, where it was currently non-existant.

Dr. Maddox approached them sporting a green, red, and white jagged striped lab coat.

"Lizzy." He shook her hand with a smile. Quick as lightning, he pounced on Joe and got him in a headlock.

"How ya doin', Joe?" he asked as he rubbed his knuckles on Joe's scalp.

"Great," replied Joe, staring blankly at the floor, a smile pasted in his face, waiting for Maddox to stop.

After a moment, Maddox released him. "So, what are y'all doing here?"

"Busted breaker," Lizzy answered. "Lab 1."

Maddox tsked. "Well, better let y'all get to it. Stop by on the way out, I'll be in my office." Maddox walked away, shoes clicking on the tiles. Lizzy and Joe looked at each other.

Lizzy began with an apologetic glance.

Joe answered with an annoyed glare at the retreating Maddox followed by a shrug.

Lizzy chuckled.

Joe gave her a look of resignation.

Lizzy ended the conversation with a pat on Joe's shoulder and a head lean towards the laboratories.

The two walked down to the end of the main corridor, through the doors, and took the first door on the left.

It was a janitor's storage closet. It also contained the breaker boxes for the laboratories. Lizzy turned on the light and told Joe to go to it. Joe took the bag and got the work. Lizzy kept watch of his progress by the door.

"You're going to work it hot?" Lizzy asked after a moment.

"Yeah," Joe replied. "Going parallel and switching boxes is too much trouble for a breaker."

Lizzy reached inside the room and pulled a wooden cane from beside the doorway.

"OK," she said. "You're the boss." The room was quiet for a while.

"Hey Lizzy?" Joe began.

"Yeah?"

"It's my birthday next week."

Lizzy smiled. "That's great, Joe! What do you want?"

Joe paused. "It's a year to my sixteenth birthday."

Lizzy's smile faded. "Yes."

Joe kept his eyes fixed on the breakers. "Am I leaving here in a year?"

Lizzy leaned against the doorframe. "Erin and I are working on that, Joe. You know we want you to get a job here."

"I know." Joe's fingers were gentle as he secured the wires and screwed the bolts back on the door.

"You do want to stay, right?" Lizzy asked.

Joe turned his head and stared in disbelief, eyebrow raised.

"OK, OK, I had to ask." Lizzy said, raising her hands.

The rest of the job was done in silence. Joe finally dropped the screwdriver into the bag and closed the panel with a snap.

Lizzy leaned out the door and looked in the next room. "Good job, the lights are on. Ready for some movies?"

Joe's usually stoic expression brightened. "Yeah. Let's stop at Miss Bea's first. I'm hungry."

After turning off the lights in the closet, they walked to Lab 4.

Dr. Beatrice Gilbert was running the tabletop centrifuge. Bea was a stocky woman with long cornrow braids arranged in a bun shape. She was the laboratory's gossip mill and played most of the single men like harps. Today she had her orange, black and green print labcoat.

"You have that nightmare coat on again, Bea?" Lizzy teased.

Bea looked up, ready to lay-in with a well-turned phrase, until she saw that it was Lizzy. "Hey, girl!" She walked around the counter to embrace her. "I thought you'd forgotten about me!"

"My dearest Bea? Never!"

Bea turned to Joe. "Hey, Mr. Man." She gave Joe a hug. "You're in luck. I have some Peanut Butter and Macadamia Nut cookies in my locker. They're all for you. You eat my chocolate, though, I'll have to kill you." She laughed out loud. Lizzy loved hearing her laugh.

Joe gave her a rare smile. "Yes, Miss Bea." He turned and headed for the door.

Bea watched him walk out. "He doesn't smile much, does he?"

"If you were the only teenager in the middle of the desert living with babies and adult women, I don't think you'd smile much either."

Bea shook her head. "Least he's being cared for. He's a good kid."

Lizzy looked past the door fondly. "Yes, he is." She turned back to Bea. "So, how's your man?"

Bea looked at her blankly. "Which one?"

Lizzy laughed out loud. "The guy in Receiving...ummm...Paul?"

"Oh." Bea wrinkled her nose. "Him. He's too possessive."

"Bea, there is kind of a limited number of available men here, y'know."

"I know," she huffed, pouting. Then she looked up and grinned evily. "Marcus still thinks you're pretty cute."

"No."

"Aw, come on!"

Lizzy rolled her eyes. "God what is this, junior high school? Do you have a note from him, too? Do I have to check a box if I like him or not?"

"What? He's cute!"

"I'm not getting booked for that."

"You're killin' me. Who's to know?"

"Shit..." Lizzy muttered. She threw Bea a look. "I wouldn't care if he was Mr. Fuckin' Universe, no way."

Bea gave a great sigh. "Oh, well," she said. "More for me."

"Happy to oblige," Lizzy said with a smile.

Lizzy's next stop was the Processing Room, or Lab 6. This was where experiments were performed with Infected materials, like blood and body tissues. Lizzy often wondered where the materials came from, but she knew better than to ask. Lizzy felt slightly nauseous in that room, but it was nothing an anacid couldn't temper.

There was another reason Lizzy needed to be careful in that particular room. Lab 6 was like all the others with one exception: a special apartment had been installed for Barry's comfort.

Barry Kruger had the dubious honor of being possessed no less than seven times since Infusion. No one could explain why: he just seemed to be more susceptible than the average human.

Barry had always been slight of build, but in the past year his condition had been deteriorating--Lizzy had even noticed a wheelchair in the lab the last time she visited. It was too bad, too, because Barry was genuinely a nice guy. Quiet, unassuming...went to services every Sunday and prayed for God's intervention. When he was in better condition he liked to play chess and boasted of being the state champion in the 100 meter dash in his senior year. He had a wife and two children that disappeared after his first possession, and he still had hopes they would be found one day. And even through all of the tests and pain and dead-ends, he was optimistic a vaccine could be found. She thought Barry would have broke the last time when they cut off his hand without anesthetic, but Barry proved tenacious.

*Bully for him...yeesh...*Lizzy shivered.

Since Barry might be in there, she checked the minature traffic light to the left of the door. It was yellow. He was in there, but not Infected.

Lizzy reached into her pocket and grabbed her pill case. Even clean, Barry had been Infected so many times he had a residual "aura." Lizzy extracted two pills and swallowed them. She would still feel like shit, but these would keep her from vomiting. Lab 6 was at the end of a hallway blocked by two sets of doors. Both required security codes in and out. She worked her way through the doors and finally entered the lab. She saw Mike Donovan and a few of his assistants, but Barry was nowhere in sight.

Mike looked like a computer geek on steroids. He carried a pocket protector and wore BCGs. His unruly brown hair reached and stretched in all directions. His build underneath his purple lab coat, though, was something any bodybuilder would envy. He was a strange combination of svelte and dorky. He saw Lizzy and grinned.

"Ah, you couldn't stand to be away from me. It's OK, all the women adore me. I'm used to it."

Lizzy grinned back. He put on such an egomaniacal front, and she loved him for it. She considered Mike the older brother she never had. Of course, the sexual innuendos were far from brotherly, but they were dry as paper. He loved his wife, Jessica, and they were all friends.

"Indeed," replied Lizzy, deadpan. "It's true. I can barely resist you."

Mike actually puffed up like a Bandy rooster. "So," he said. "Is the breaker fixed in Lab 1?"

"Yup. How's the latest theory panning out?"

"Actually, this is pretty cool..." Mike began, and then dunked Lizzy in a thick, bubbly stew of syntax that contained chunky words like "T-cells," "Autoimmune," and "Cytoplast."

This was typical Mike: before Infusion, he was a scientist in a secret federal laboratory that specialized in biological warfare. He was highly successful, because Mike approached bacteria and viruses with the same enthusiasm as a sociopathic nine-year-old would with the world's supply of gerbils and cherry bombs. What tended to disturb people most was he didn't care whether he was creating viruses or destroying them--it was all the same to him. What got him off was the whole scientific process and its end result.

He was also trained as a surgeon, and a brilliant one at that, but it was his amoral the-cities-are-burning-Whee! attitude that compromised Mike's bedside manner and kept him in the laboratory and not working with patients:

"Well, Mrs. Smith, you've contracted flesh-eating bacteria. Here's some great blowup pictures of the cell degeneration on your arm now, and here's what I think it'll look like in two months! Can't even see the epidermis anymore—isn't that neat? Mind if we take pictures once a day for research purposes? Don't get upset, you'll be able to see them, if that's what you're worried about..."

Lizzy nodded during Mike's *soup du jour* in all the right places, but the bottom line of what he was saying was the same as it had been for the last five years: the scientists thought the demons took over the body in a similar fashion as a virus, and there had to be an anti-virus somewhere and they *really* close this time...

Suddenly Lizzy realized Mike had stopped talking and was looking at her expectantly. Lizzy snapped herself out of her stupor and said, "I'm just glad you're the scientist."

Mike nodded and smiled, falling for her fake. "So, want to stay for dinner? They're having Chicken in Wine Sauce."

"Nah. I have the 8-12s tonight."

Mike snorted. "Blow it off!"

"I can't just blow it off!"

"Sure you can!"

"Break things more often, I could be here every day."

"Fine," Mike sighed, sounding dejected. "Go back to your dyke friends. It's OK."

Lizzy wouldn't be baited. "Oh, I'll dream of you tonight." Her voice was teasing, but her eyes said, *"That's enough, Mike."*

Mike's eyes drained of sarcasm and he understood the look. The only thing that saved Mike was that he knew when to quit--most of the time.

"All right. Next time, then. Jess would like to see you."

Lizzy nodded. "I'll try. Where's Barry, by the way?"

"Sleeping. Do you need to see him?"

"No. Just wanted to say hi."

"I'll tell him you were here." Mike bent over a petri dish. "Might not want to wait too long to see him, Liz," he said, not looking up.

"I know," Lizzy replied. "Good luck with the project."

"See ya," Mike said absently, absorbed in his work.

Lizzy finally caught up with Joe at the 8mm room. "What did you find, Joe?"

Joe looked at the DVDs in his hand and began reading in his classic monotone. "'American Pie,' 'A Fistful of Dollars,' 'Enter the Dragon...'"

"Joe," Lizzy interrupted. "Did you happen to remember you don't live by yourself out there? The other seventy-five women you live with? Hmmm?"

Joe smirked and kept reading like she hadn't interrupted him. "'An Affair to Remember,' 'All About Eve,' 'Like Water for Chocolate,' 'Bram Stoker's Dracula...'"

"OK," Lizzy interruped again. "Great taste as always. No one knows the feminine mystique better than you, Casanova. Be sure to get children's movies, too."

Joe turned his head and read the titles from the DVDs from his other hand. "'The Sword in the Stone,' 'The Swan Princess,' 'Scooby Doo Meets Frankenstein...'"

"All right, smart ass," Lizzy broke in again, smiling. "Have you gone to the library yet?"

"I dropped off the returns, but I haven't filled the requests yet."

"Want to do lunch first?"

"Sure."

It was about 1500 before they left the lab. Joe slipped his blindfold back on. Lizzy found a NWA tape in the glove compartment.

"Y'know," Lizzy shouted over the music as they drove back to Ruth. "I remember when I used to listen to Enya, The Doors, Metallica..."

Joe smirked but didn't answer. He was reclining in his seat, tapping his foot. Lizzy guessed he was reminiscing about the streets of Chicago, playing with his childhood friends.

After Lizzy parked the truck at the motor pool, she decided to pay a visit to the child center. As Lizzy approached the building, a dark-haired child ran up to meet her.

"Aunt Lizzy! Aunt Lizzy!" he yelled.

"Brydan!" Lizzy caught him and tossed him over her shoulder. "How's my favorite godchild?"

Brydan giggled and punched Lizzy in the back with tiny fists. She walked with him perched on her shoulder the rest of the way to the center.

"Put me down! Put me down, Aunt Lizzy!" Brydan protested between peals of laughter.

"Never!" Lizzy answered, spinning around.

Brydan shrieked with delight.

"Oh, all right!" Lizzy put Brydan down and took his hand. "What have you been up to?"

"We all had dinner and Joey won't give me my truck and...and Allison got sick and Mommy said she needed to stop eating so much and..."

They reached the door and Lizzy opened it for him. "In you go."

"...I want to watch Barney and...and...do you think we could?" Brydan finished.

"We'll see," Lizzy replied. "Where's your Mommy?"

"I'll get her!" Brydan ran into the next room.

Lizzy could hear "Mommy! Mommy!" followed by a gentle *shush*ing. "Mommy, Aunt Lizzy's here!" Brydan reported in a stage whisper.

A chair creaked, and Brydan ran back into the room followed by Mary. A very pregnant Mary.

"Hi, Mare," said Lizzy, givng to her friend a shallow hug over the protruding stomach.

"Hello!" Mary replied.

"Have the night shift?"

"Yup."

"I'm surprised they gave you the night watch."

"Actually, it makes sense. They put me in charge of the four and five-year-olds, and they sleep through the night, mostly. Besides, I'm sleeping in chairs now, and not too often. Doesn't matter when I work, really. *Ummph.*"

Mary grimaced with discomfort. She waddled to a rocking chair and eased into it. Lizzy sat across from her and pulled Brydan into her lap.

"Wasn't that kid dropping soon?" Lizzy asked.

"Any day now." Mary winced as the fetus kicked. "Good things take time," she said, smiling, caressing her stomach.

"Hope so," Lizzy answered. "He's been an active one."

"Can't wait."

"How are the other ones?"

"Catherine is starting to crawl. Daniel was running around the nursery the last time I saw him, a terror." Mary paused while the fetus kicked again. She smiled the secret smile only those with child can do.

Brydan squrimed out of Lizzy's lap and ran into the next room.

"Jennifer continues to say "NO!" to everything, Matty won't eat anything green, yellow, or red, and Brydan..." Mary motioned to the next room. "Hyper as ever."

"We got new movies today."

"That's nice." Mary looked out the screen door. "You know who I thought about yesterday? Phillip Bergman."

"Phil? God..." Lizzy leaned back and smiled. "Mr. Football Player, Honor Roll, yearbook, *allll* that..."

"He thought he was It..." Mary giggled.

"I still remember what he looked like in his football uniform. Especially his legs. I don't know what it was about them..."

"I don't think anything about that guy's looks was a mistake," Mary commented. "You know he probably groomed himself for hours..."

Lizzy smiled. "Mmm! Why are you thinking about him? He completely ignored two band-os like us."

"One of the boys here looks like him."

"Really? Who?"

"Melissa's oldest, Jason. Want to take a look?"

"Sure."

Lizzy helped Mary out of her chair and walked with her into the next rooms.

The childcare center and the clinic were the only two buildings at the commune with actual walls and a roof. The childcare building was shaped like a giant doughnut, with an opened canvas-covered courtyard in the center. The building's semi-permanent sides separated easily, so they could be loaded on huge flatbeds for transport. The rooms were side by side with no long hallways or doors; the only doors were to the infant nursery on the Northeast corner, and they were always closed. This meant the children could run from room to room, room to courtyard, and back again during playtime.

Between those who were scheduled to be at the center, and the mommies spending time with children, there was an average of twenty women on the site during the day. All the women took equal responsibility for raising the children. Quibbles sometimes ensued over differing discipline philosophies, but the communal way worked at Ruth. The kids were happy, oblivious to the fact that their way of life wasn't anything like how their mothers and the other women were raised.

Brydan had been the first child born at Ruth, before the ultrasound equipment or even the vital sign monitors arrived. He was a bright child, and recently begun to ask where the grown men were, why they never went anywhere, and where babies came from. Mary had gone to Erin, and the last time Lizzy had asked, the two were still hashing out an explanation that the child could understand, that wouldn't give him nightmares, and yet would be some semblance of the truth. That was two weeks ago, and Lizzy guessed they were still working on it.

Lizzy supposed the surviving government hadn't printed that particular manual yet.

Three rooms later, Lizzy and Mary found Jason. He was with three other children, playing with blocks on the floor. They both looked at the child.

"What do you think?" Mary asked.

Lizzy walked around the child. "Same hair, the legs are a little too chubby..."

60

"Lizzy!" Mary exclaimed. "Be serious..."

Lizzy huffed in mock disgruntlement. "All right," and squatted down to look at the kid's face. Jason looked up at Lizzy. Lizzy smiled at him and winked. Jason grinned, and then reached down and silently began to give Lizzy red block, then a blue one, then a yellow one...

"Maybe it's a Mommy thing," Lizzy said to Mary, taking the blocks and stacking them in front of Jason like the walls of the little fort, "but I don't see how this four-year-old looks like Phillip the last time we saw him."

"Look at his head," Mary said.

Lizzy stopped building the wall and focused on Jason's scalp. Right on the hairline above the right eye was a large red birthmark.

"And?" Lizzy asked, looking at it. Jason reached over and knocked the wall down with a sweep of his chubby fist. He giggled.

"I knew Phillip in elementary school, and his Dad made him get crew cuts until high school. He had a birthmark that looked exactly like that."

Lizzy stood and turned to Mary. "Could be a coincidence."

"Yes," Mary agreed. "Do you know what happened to Phillip after high school? I don't."

Lizzy thought. "He went to Dartmouth. That's the last I heard about him. Maybe he donated to a sperm bank and the government got a hold of it."

"Maybe." They both stood there, looking at Jason.

# ✦CHAPTER TEN✦

*Commune Ruth*
*"Courtesy Tent"*
*Two Weeks Later*
*0315*

Lizzy was sitting on a folding chair under a lit-up tarp, squinting at sheet music lying on a card table. She was strumming chords experimentally on her traveling guitar when she heard the gate *creak-creak-creak* open and saw Anna slip out.
*Dammit--didn't we just oil that gate?*
Anna was dressed in light blue scrubs and sneakers. Lizzy noticed that her hair was different--it was a short bob now, rather than long and in a ponytail. She looked tired.
"Hey, Anna. What's going on?"
"Nothing much." Anna looked around. "Where's your other watchstander?"
Lizzy nodded over at a far corner. "Pam's over there. I'm working on the Christmas Cantata music."
Anna looked in the corner. She saw a lump on the ground, wrapped in a blanket. It appeared to be breathing.
Lizzy asked, "What are you doing up so late?" She gestured with the neck of her guitar towards a second folding chair.
Anna sighed and sank into it. "Thanks. Sarah Gilmore delivered tonight. A baby boy, though he was blue when they pulled him out. We don't know what's going to happen."
"Jesus," Lizzy said. "How's Sarah?"
"Crushed," Anna replied. "OK, physically. He pinked up when they gave him oxygen, and his APGAR was much better after the ten minutes, but we're not sure how long he was deprived."
Lizzy stared out into the desert night. There was no sound except for the *eep-eep-eep* of the night insects, and the occasional snore from Pam. The infant mortality rate at Ruth was quite low, thanks to Master Chief, but they still had maybe two babies a year stillbirth or die soon after delivery. Ill or damaged babies, maybe another one or two a year, were sent to Headquarters for evaluation; about half of them, the ones with no long-term damage, returned. The mothers of the other babies were sent official notices that their babies did not survive. Anna always had her hands full ministering to those mothers: Lizzy never considered how important having a body to hold and bury could be. As it was, Anna always took pictures of the critical babies with their mothers before they shipped them off, in case the worst happened. That, at least, seemed to be a small comfort. Still, Lizzy once had to hold Mary while a two-week-old Jennifer was packed in a medical van and sent to HQ; she would rather be in a roomful of Infected than hear those screams and wails ever again.
"Anna," Lizzy began. "Why don't the mothers run?"
Anna looked at her. "What?"
"Have you ever had a mother that has lost a child run away into the Wilderness?"

Anna considered. "I've had two mothers that have lost babies and run, but never right away--not like you'd think. All of the women who have run, there seemed to be no rhyme or reason--they just left. No triggering event, which is what's so weird about it."

"What do you mean?"

"When people commit suicide, or go into a depression, there is usually something called a Triggering Event--something bad happened, and they react. Or, sometimes when someone decides to commit suicide, they'll look like they're getting better, when actually they have just made up their mind, and they feel better. Whenever I counsel anyone after people run, though, they almost always say that it was business as usual, nothing unusual. One minute they're here, the next they're gone."

Lizzy considered this. "Well, we've only lost four people so far. What do you think is going on?"

Anna shook her head. "I don't know. Something we don't see."

The two women sat in silence for a while. Finally, Anna said, "Why don't you run?"

"What do you mean?"

"You never get enough sleep. You have no children to keep you here. You hate the military. Why not take your chances?"

Lizzy looked at her. "Are we talking about you or me here?"

Anna leaned back and looked up at the canvas ceiling. Her mouth twitched a little.

"Why don't you run, Liz?"

Lizzy suddenly felt her stomach drop. This conversation just got very, very serious, and she felt very inadequate to the task. She considered her answer for a few moments before she spoke.

"I suppose there are two reasons. As hard as life is here, every so often I get to leave and go somewhere else for a while. For those who can't leave, who have nowhere to go, I don't know how they manage it. That would drive me raving mad, only seeing this place everyday. I suppose most folks have children to keep them occupied, but I really don't know."

Anna looked back over and considered her. She did get to go to HQ twice a year. "OK. What's your second reason?"

"If I committed suicide, how would I know what the hell happened next?"

"That's it?"

Lizzy shrugged. "It's gotten me through a lot. This life has been a wild ride, Anna. Don't you want to see what happens next?"

Anna looked into the desert and sighed. "I suppose so."

"It sucks here. But it might get better." Lizzy reached over and turned some pages of sheet music, not looking at Anna, and not knowing what else to say. "Here--I've been working on this second piece. Let me know what you think."

She began to play. Anna listened.

◆　◆　◆　◆

"Push, Mare!"

"FUCK YOU, BITCH!"

Lizzy smiled. Mare only swore when she was in the third phase of labor. They've been doing this for so long, it was as if they were following a pre-prepared script.

Master Chief Johnson was watching the action on the other side of the drape. "OK, Mary, we've got a crown--you're doing great! Three, two, one--OK!"

Mary stopped pushing and panted. "Are we...almost done? Please...tell me... we're almost done!"

Master Chief looked at the monitors, and then back down. "I think one more should do it. And...PUSH!"

Mary took a deep breath and strained.

"Almost, almost, al-most..." Master Chief leaned back a little as Mary exhaled in a *whoosh.* "Gotcha!"

Two seconds later, the sound of baby cry filled the air. Mary began to laugh and cry with relief.

Master Chief smiled. "Congratulations, Mary!" he yelled over the howling. "He's beautiful, and a healthy pink!"

Mary smiled through her sobbing. "Thank you, Chris."

Master Chief handed the writhing pink baby to Taz, a HS3/8. "OK, Mary. Ready for the rest?"

A short while later, Lizzy was sitting on Mary's bed in sick bay, watching the newborn giving nursing his first go. "Wow, another natural latcher, Mare."

Mare winced and looked down at the tiny baby. "Why does it *always* hurt at first? I've been nursing for almost six years; you'd think we'd all be used to it by now."

"No idea, Mare." Lizzy knew from talking to other nursing women that pain for the first couple of weeks was not unusual. "He really is beautiful, though."

Mary smiled. "Yes, he is. Perfect APGAR, couldn't ask for more."

"Glad it's over?" Each mother was required to birth five children. Mary was the first at Commune Ruth to reach that goal.

"Right now, no--you know I always want another one right after delivery. Ask me again in a couple of weeks, when I'm not sleeping. How are the kids?"

"I checked while they were cleaning you up. I told them they had a new baby brother. Brydan was disappointed--you know he really wanted a girl. The rest of the kids were kind of indifferent."

"They'll love him. They always do." The baby had fallen asleep; Mary delatched him and settled him into the crook of her arm. He snored softly. "I have great kids."

"Yes, you do." Lizzy noted the baby's light skin and curly black hair. "I can't tell yet how much he looks like you."

"I think he has my nose."

"I think he does," Lizzy agreed. "So, what shall we call him?"

Mary smiled. "You really like this part, don't you?"

"Yeah!" Lizzy replied, smiling. "It can make or break a kid. Besides, it's one of the few creative things we can do around here."

"True, true." Mary transferred the baby to her other arm. The baby slept

64

on. "Well, we had talked about Nicholas, after my Pap-Pap."

Lizzy looked at the baby for a moment. The sun pored through weather-beaten Plexiglas, and the dust motes gave the light a hazy, filtered look. Still, she could see the baby clearly in his mother's arms.

"That's a good name. It fits him."

"What's his middle name, Liz?"

This was a tradition between the two women--Lizzy had given each of Mary's children their middle names. She knew what she wanted to say, but she still pondered for a few moments to be sure.

"How about Adams? I got done reading the book about John Adams a couple of months ago, and the guy never got enough credit."

"Nicholas Adams Shapiro," Mary said. "I like it."

"Cool. Thank you, Mary."

"No, Lizzy." Mary looked up, and Lizzy saw she was going to cry again--she'd be on a roller coaster of hormones for at least a day. "Thank you. If you hadn't called me, I wouldn't be here, and I wouldn't have my children."

Lizzy held out her arms, and she almost teared up, too. "Ah, shucks. Why don't you give Nicky to me, Mommy, and you can get some rest. The man and I are going to see the town."

Mary gave Nicholas to Lizzy, and then settled back into the pillows and closed her eyes. "No girls, no booze, Aunt Lizzy."

Lizzy grinned as she sat in the recliner next to the bed, arranging Nicholas on her shoulder. He squirmed a little, but Lizzy patted his back, and he settled back down. "Not now, maybe later."

# ·CHAPTER ELEVEN·

*Three Months Later*
*In the Desert*
*06 A.I.*

Lizzy sat in the driver's seat of the truck, throwing dust plumes in her wake as she sped down the road, blaring Metallica's "Unforgiven." She was alone this trip--Joe had a test to take in Algebra II that morning.

Today was Lizzy's birthday, and that meant a very special present from Bea. She gave Lizzy the same present every year, and Erin never seemed to notice that something always broke on this particular day every year. (Something, of course, that could be fixed easily.) And no one noticed that Lizzy always came back late this one date every year.

*Or, maybe no one cares...*

Lizzy weaved around the deserted town and came to a stop by the front gate. Larry was there, as usual.

"Hi, Larry." Lizzy greeted.

"Ili, Lizzy. Something broken again?"

"Just a centrifugue. Simple wiring problem, they think. What do you need today?"

Larry checked his clipboard. The requirements changed every so often.

"The name of this town," Larry said.

Lizzy got out her notebook and pen and wrote, "I have no idea." She showed it to him.

"Yup, Come on in." If she had known the name of the town, and the demons probably did from the earliest Infusions, it wasn't Lizzy.

Lizzy stepped through the gate and went inside. It was quiet as usual, and Lizzy went to Bea's lab.

"Hi!" Bea greeted with a huge smile. "I thought you'd run out here."

"Only to see you, Bea," Lizzy replied, giving Bea a hug. "Nothing to do with my present."

"Yeah, right!" Bea shoved her away. She began to pout.

Lizzy decided to play the game. She sided up to Bea and put her arm around her shoulders. "Who loves you, Bea?"

Bea glanced at Lizzy, looked back down, and kept pouting, trying to hide a smile.

"Not you," she muttered, looking down at the floor.

Lizzy began to rock Bea back and forth from foot to foot. "C'mon..." she said soothingly, "Who's my favorite mad scientist?"

Bea giggled. "Oh, all right!" Bea pulled away and went to her drawer. She opened it and pulled out a small box. "Happy Birthday, Liz." She handed Lizzy the box.

Once opened, Lizzy found two small pills. "How many mg?"

"Enough that you'll feel nothing," Bea answered, grinning.

Lizzy tossed them back in her mouth and swallowed them. "One day a year, no responsibilities," she said, eyes closed.

"My pleasure," said Bea. "Now fix my damn centrifuge before you fuzz out."

An hour later, Lizzy felt great. She had no worries, no problems, and everyone was *cool...*

"I'm goin' ta see Mike and Jess," Lizzy said, slurring slightly and grinning from ear to ear.

"OK..." said Bea, hesitating. "Just don't talk to anyone else, OK?"

"You betcha." She walked out of the room and headed to Lab 6.

She stopped at the door and checked the traffic light. It was green--Barry wasn't there.

Lizzy punched the codes and walked in the lab. It was empty. Pristine, quiet, empty.

Lizzy looked around, and then noticed an electric cord on a table lamp had a deep cut. Wires of different colors were peaking out.

*Easy fix*, Lizzy thought, and reached in her toolbelt for a roll of electrical tape.

In her stoned absorption, she didn't hear the door click open, or Barry coming in. He walked toward Lizzy, smiling.

Lizzy heard his footsteps and looked up.

"Hi, Barry!" she said, smiling back. *Barry is cool...*

Barry smiled back and waved. He came along side and put his arm around her waist. She put her arm around his shoulder and squeezed a silent greeting.

As she felt his bony hand cup her side and press in a half-hug, she felt a needle slide underneath her ribs.

*Pow.*

"OUCH! What the..." Lizzy yelped, pulling away. Then she really looked at Barry.

Barry just stood there, a skeleton with tufts of thinning red hair and yellow skin. He was smiling at her with his grey lips and rotten teeth as a small hypodermic needle gun flashed in his left claw. Lizzy reached for the taser she kept strapped to her left thigh.

Then she realized to her horror her fingers wouldn't curl around the handle. In fact, she could barely move her left arm at all. From the other side of the room she heard pounding on the door and muffled shouting.

*"WHAT THE FUCK DID YOU DO?"* she screamed. Her legs began to buckle. With her last remaining strength she took a deep breath and shrieked before her body sank to the floor.

Seconds later, Mike and half the lab rushed in from the hallway. Maggie, one of Mike's assistants, stopped in her tracks and retched.

"He's hot!" she shouted. "I knew it!"

Five people tackled Barry to the floor. "Watch the needle!" someone shouted. "What the hell is with the hypogun?" another yelled.

Lizzy was watching the commotion through frozen eyes. She saw Mike bending over her, checking her pulse. His face was pale; his usual amused expression was gone, replaced by serious concentration. He was sweating.

*He's scared*, she thought.

*I'm fucked.*

She started to see spots in her field of vision and was finding it harder and harder to breathe.

"Why the hell is she dying?" Mike asked aloud. "She shouldn't be dying from Infusion..."

"She's not," Maggie interrupted. "She's clean."

"You sure?" He was already pointing at Barry. "What's in the hypo?"

One of the assistants examined the vial in the gun. "Vimulant," he read.

"Fuck." Mike started fumbling, trying to unbutton Lizzy's shirt. "How much?"

"The whole vial."

Mike grabbed her shirt with both hands and ripped. Buttons flew. The voices and faces were getting farther away from Lizzy as she struggled to take breaths.

"Get the Adrenol now!" Mike yelled over his shoulder.

Lizzy heard glass breaking in the distance, and feet thumping on the floor.

"OK, Lizzy," Mike said in a calm voice as he unbuckled her tool belt and unbuttoned her work pants. "This is really going to suck."

Someone handed him a gun with the fattest, longest needle Lizzy had ever seen.

"Here we go." Mike slammed the needle home, and Lizzy's chest exploded with pain. She managed a grunt.

Mike pulled the trigger. Nothing happened. Looking confused, he crouched down and examined the gun.

Then he grinned. In in instant, the old Mike was back. "Oh yeah, right," he said to himself. He clicked off the safety switch, and looked into Lizzy's eyes. She saw him waving at her with one hand, smiling, as he pulled the trigger again with the other.

The hypogun fired. Lizzy passed out.

# ·CHAPTER TWELVE·

*Several Hours Later*

When Lizzy awoke, she was in one of the lab's private sickrooms. Like the rest of the lab, it was quiet, white, and sterile. A picture of dogs smoking around the table and playing cards on the opposite wall. An IV bag was dripping clear solution down a clear tube and into a needle in her arm. Her chest throbbed. Her eyes felt dried out. She felt like shit.

Mike and Jessica were sitting next to her bed. Mike was grinning from ear to ear. He pointed at Lizzy.

"You owe me!" he crowed, bouncing in his chair.

Lizzy sighed and tried her voice. "Yes, Mike, thank you," she croaked.

Mike was downright bubbly. "So, how do you feel?"

Lizzy gave Mike a look. "I feel like...someone who got stabbed...in the heart with 250cc of Adrenol." She gestured to a water pitcher sitting on a table next to the bed. Jessica pored a cup of water and handed it to her.

"I also gave you shots of Mynacodrozine 10 and Jeff's Cocktail."

*Jeff's Cocktail?* Lizzy leaned back. Mike liked something about Jeff's Cocktail. Then she remembered...and winced. "Great. I get to turn bluish-green..."

Mike grinned wider and nodded. "I also gave you something to counteract Bea's present."

Lizzy and Jessica froze. Jessica lifted an eyebrow and silently looked from Mike to Lizzy.

The corners of Lizzy's mouth twitched. She purposely kept her eyes on Mike's face. "I'm glad I told you about that. Did anyone find out?"

Mike shook his head, and then wiggled his eyebrows. "You owe me!"

"Gee, Mike," Lizzy sighed again. "How-can-I-ever-thank-you?"

Mike smiled at her wickedly. "Well..." He rolled his eyes around like he was considering the question. "I don't know..." Then Mike caught a glance of Jessica's icy stare and her raised eyebrows, and he physically flinched.

"Your eternal gratitude will be fine," he said, not missing a beat. He blinked at Jessica innocently.

"So," Lizzy asked, trying to save Mike. "What happened to Barry?"

Mike's eyes instantly drained of their mirth and filled with lead. "We couldn't save him this time. We had to put him down."

Lizzy looked at Mike in disbelief that he actually said that. "'Put him down?' You make him sound like a lab animal."

Mike shrugged in indifference. "Better than trying to exorcise him again. We would've had to amputate again, probably. More humane this way."

Lizzy nodded in agreement. He had a point. "That's too bad. He was a nice guy."

"Mmmm..." Mike grunted and was looking at the ceiling, now lost in his own thoughts. "Now I have to find another Demon Whore...God, they're hard to find..."

Lizzy looked at him. "Hey, Mike?" Mike looked up at her.

"You're a sadistic motherfucker."

Mike grinned and his eyes lit up. "Yeah," he drawled, pointing at Lizzy again. "You owe me!"

"All right," Jessica said, getting up. "That's enough." She pulled Mike up by his shoulders and guided him to the door. "I need to ask Lizzy some questions before she sleeps again."

"We'll talk about paybacks later!" Mike called on the way out, waving. Lizzy waved back as the door closed behind him. Jessica walked back to Lizzy's bedside and sat down. In addition to being Mike's wife, she was also the lab's psychiatrist and demon behavioral expert. She told Lizzy once she had been recruited by the government a few years before Infusion, but she would never talk about why or what she did. Whatever it was, though, it made Jessica very sad. Most of the time, though, it seemed she was too busy with her work or looking after Mike to dwell on it.

"Are you all right to talk?" Jessica asked.

"Yes," Lizzy replied.

Jessica took off her glasses and looked Lizzy in the eyes. "What...'present'?"

"Who's asking?"

"The psychiatrist."

Lizzy looked at her blankly. "Hmmm...I don't know what Mike was talking about. You'll have to ask him."

Jessica sighed and looked at the opposite wall. Lizzy knew this was the last thing she wanted to do.

"All right," Jessica replied. "Who should ask?"

Lizzy smiled. "My priest."

"Goddammit," Jessica muttered. "No, no, no, I'm not doing that." She rubbed her temples. She sighed. "Look, I know what you want, but I need to sleep at night. I'm your friend, Liz. If you're using drugs, I have to be able to help you get the right treatments, not to mention my obligations as a doctor."

Lizzy nodded. When Jessica got into "shrink mode", she sometimes forgot that Lizzy wasn't stupid. Priests don't let infractions end up in your service jacket, and they keep their mouths shut.

"Just let me know when Father Jess arrives."

Jessica glared at Lizzy. She put her glasses back on and took out a notebook and pen. "What happened in the lab?"

Lizzy explained the episode, her eyes never leaving her hands that were folded on the blanket. Jessica took notes. When Lizzy was done, they both sat in silence.

Lizzy finally spoke again. "It was planned."

"Yes," Jessica agreed.

More silence. "*They don't plan,*" Lizzy pointed out.

"No," Jessica agreed again. "I've never heard of anything like this."

"Why me?"

"I don't know. Piss off any demons lately?"

Lizzy shook her head. "I haven't encountered face-to-face since Newport. What happened to 'mindless animals?'"

"I'll be making some radio calls after I'm done here. Maybe this isn't a new thing and the information just hasn't hit the weeds yet. What I don't get is, why didn't they just posess you?"

Lizzy considered that. "Can they? Maybe it has to do with my being a Sensor."

"No," Jessica said. "It has nothing to do with posession. I think they wanted you plain dead. Sorry," added Jessica, seeing the depressed look on Lizzy's face.

Lizzy suddenly looked up. "When you make your radio calls, ask about anyone who was in Newport, particularly William Bryant and Dr....Hart. Donald Hart, I think?"

Jessica wrote the names down. "Shouldn't be hard. There has been limited demon activity over the past 18 months."

Lizzy was surprised. "Really?"

Jessica nodded, not looking up from her note-taking. "Only one outpost has fallen this year. Very quiet."

"What does that mean?"

Jessica shrugged. She kept writing. "Some think with the populations so dispersed as they are, it just isn't 'fun' anymore." Jessica paused. "Some think there's more to it, but I try not to think about it." She looked up at Lizzy.

"'Cause if I did think about the possibilities, I'd never shit again." She bent her head again. "All right, my child, I will now hear your confession."

"Ah, absolution," Lizzy sighed. "It's a beautiful thing."

◆　◆　◆　◆

Four days later, Lizzy climbed back into her truck and drove back to the outpost. Erin met her at the motor pool.

"Jesus, Lizzy," she began as Lizzy eased out of her truck. "Quite the celebrity, huh?"

"What do you mean?"

"I got a radio call from Headquarters. Next month, they're gathering all the OINCs and Official Sensors on account of you."

Lizzy tried to look apologetic. "Where?"

"At Headquarters," she said. She looked at Lizzy accusingly.

Lizzy stared at her. "What?"

Erin looked away. "Nothin'..." She started to walk away.

"What?" Lizzy began to chase her. "How was I supposed to prevent this?" she called, gaining. "This isn't my damn fault. By the way, I'm much better, thanks."

Erin stopped and turned around. Her gaze softened a little. "Sorry, Liz. I'm glad to see you're all right. It just...figures this would happen to you."

Lizzy held up her hands. "Sorry." She looked at Erin. "Is there something else going on? You're freaking out way too much over this."

Erin crossed her arms and looked away at the mountains. She was muttering to herself, like she was rehearsing a speech.

*She's choosing her words,* Lizzy realized.

She looked back at Lizzy. "For the past five years I've run a quiet outpost. I've filed my reports on time, no one questions them, and no one interferes with my operation. Not all commune OINCs are that lucky. I just hope this doesn't get people too curious about the place, y'know?"

"Sure, Erin." *Bullshit...* "But I don't think Ruth will be involved. It didn't happen here. I just happen to sleep here."

Erin still looked worried, but she said, "Yeah, you're probably right. Ready to do some work?"

Lizzy looked across the desert. She sighed. *Conversation over...*

"You bet."

◆　◆　◆　◆

*Commune Ruth*

Joe approached Lizzy at breakfast. He took a spot across from her at the table, coffee in hand.

"What happened?" he asked. "You were gone for a while. You look paler than usual...or something."

"Gee, thanks," Lizzy replied. She took a sip of coffee. "Barry got infected, and I was in the room. I got roughed up a little." She lifted a forkful of eggs and chewed.

"Damn," Joe said. "What happened to Barry? Is everyone OK?"

"Barry didn't make it. Everyone else is fine," Lizzy answered with a sad smile.

"You can still go the lab, right?"

"As far as I know."

"That's good." Joe stood up. "Glad to see you're OK."

"Hey," Lizzy exclaimed, noticing Joe's cup. "Since when do you drink coffee? You'll stunt your growth."

Joe smirked and shrugged. He climbed over the bench and walked away.

An hour later, Lizzy walked to the command tent for the weekly department meeting. As Lizzy walked into the tent, BM2 Olin saw her and approached. She gave Lizzy an once-over.

"You look like shit," Olin told her. "What the fuck happened to you?"

Lizzy walked to the nearest chair and eased down into it. "I had hoped I'd look better by now. Erin hasn't told anyone what happened?"

Olin shook her head.

"I think I can safely tell you that an Infected specimen got loose, and I got in the way. Other than that, you'll have to talk to Erin--I'm not sure what I can say or not say."

Olin nodded. "Did it bite you?"

Lizzy shook her head. "I got lucky."

Olin nodded again, and then turned her back and went to her usual chair, to the right of the head, where Erin sat. Lizzy supposed that, as third in command, she should sit on Erin's left, but she never really cared about where she sat.

Though, now that she thought about it, Lizzy considered that she usually sat closest to the door when she could, facing it. Ever since she heard of the Dead Man's Hand, she always tried to sit so she could see the door.

Sitting close to the door, in these times, was just common sense.

Erin eventually came in, and all of the department heads took their seats. HSMC/10 Johnson was technically the highest ranked petty officer at the Commune; however, Boatswain's Mates or Machinery Technicians were traditionally ONICs before Infusion, and the existing government chose to continue this practice. If Master Chief was bitter about being subordinate to a second class, though, she never complained about it. Rather, she seemed to be satisfied running the clinic and serving as the Education Officer. Thanks to the diligence of Master Chief, some of the women were very close to obtaining Bachelors degrees through correspondance courses.

Erin sat down and began the meeting. "Good Morning, Ladies."

There was a rumble of "morning" in reply.

"Let's start with the XPO. Olin?"

Olin's report was nothing unusual--vaccinations this and pregnancy rate that. When Olin was finished, Erin shot a look towards Lizzy that said, *Don't you dare say anything about the lab.*

"Townsend? What's going on maintenance-wise?"

Lizzy played it straight. She said she had just returned from an extensive maintence job at the lab, but it seems the plant was fine, and she had nothing unusual to report.

Erin nodded. "Master Chief?"

About forty-five minutes later, the meeting was adjourned. Nothing about the lab incident was mentioned.

The women rose and chatted as they filed out. Lizzy walked over to where Anna was waiting in the queue to leave the tent.

Anna looked at her face. "Why are you bluish-green?"

Lizzy smiled. "A long story. How are the babies?"

"All seems well. No births scheduled for a week or so, though babies will surprise you." She paused and smiled as she moved with the line.

"Babies are never late, nor are they early. Babies arrive precisely when they mean to."

Lizzy smiled. "Babies and wizards." She waited until she and Anna shuffled through the door into the blinding sunlight to speak again. "Have you been reading Tolkien?"

"I saw the movies a while ago, but I thought I'd try out the books. Wow," Anna looked down at Liddy's gait. "You really look odd in the sunlight. Where are you going?"

"I have to check on the plant. There was an incident at the lab, but that's all I can really say about it. It'll clear up in another day or two."

"I hope so," Anna said. "You look like a sick smurf."

Liddy thought about Mike and sighed. "Yeah, that was the general idea."

# ◆CHAPTER THIRTEEN◆

*Commune Ruth*
*Main Courtyard*
*Three Weeks Later*
*0805*

"LOOK TO YOUR LEFT!" Pause.
"LOOK TO YOUR RIGHT!" Pause.
"ANYONE MISSING?"
Women raised their hands. The names were taken. Olin compared the
lists.
"Where's Verner?" Olin asked the group.
The ranks shifted. People murmured.
Polly raised her hand. "XO? I saw her late last night about 2200." She
looked like she was on the edge of panic.
Olin nodded. "Anyone else? Who's her roomate?"
A small, slight girl named Jo raised her hand. "She was..."
"I'll see you in my office after this, George," Olin interrupted. "That's all.
Dismissed."
A couple of females went to Polly's side, whisking her away to her tent.
Lizzy walked to a bench and sat down. She couldn't believe this was
happening again; she needed to think.
It wasn't unheard of for people to escape. It happened. But Lizzy knew
Steph, and Steph wasn't that unhappy. She had recently broken up with Polly, but
they split as friends. They spent more happy time with each other as pals than they
ever did as lovers.
In the beginning, before the children, it was more believable that women
would want to escape. But Steph had three children. She had kids to stay for
now.
And yet, Lizzy still wouldn't have thought twice about Steph, other than to
mourn her, but the episode with Erin when she got back from the lab didn't feel
right. Erin was hiding something. Something bad. Lizzy got the sickening feeling
that she was on the cusp of something unholy.

◆  ◆  ◆  ◆

*Commune Ruth*
*"Courtesy Tent"*
*Three Days Later*
*1145*

"Anything to pass?"
"No. Same old, same old."
Lizzy and Polly were packing up their gear and trash. Stacy and Danelle

74

were dropping their gear. They were all under the canvas canopy outside the gate, out of the desert sun. Lizzy was slinging her canteen over her head when she noticed movement out of the corner of her eye.

She pushed her sunglasses up her nose and stared near a clump of cactii about 500 yards away.

"Shit," she breathed. She grabbed Polly and turned her in the right direction. "Right in front of you, two figures."

Polly and the others squinted. "Maybe," Polly said. "Can't see that well."

Lizzy picked up the shotgun threw it to Polly and felt on her thigh for her tazer. "We'll check to out." Polly scowled at her. She ignored her. "Tell the watchtower," she said to Stacy and Danelle. To Polly she said, "Let's go."

Lizzy and Polly started the trek across the desert.

"Can you still see them?" Polly asked as they jogged.

"No. I think they took off when we started to come out here. We should be able to track them, though."

They reached the group of cactii. They spread out a little and looked around.

"I don't see anything," said Polly, looking down. "Wild goose chase, Liz..."

Lizzy studied the ground. "I think," Lizzy said, crouching down, "these are brushmarks." She pointed to wavy indentations in the sand.

Polly stared. "Want to follow them?"

Lizzy stood up. "You stay here. The others should be right behind. I'll see where these go."

Polly nodded, looking back towards the outpost. "I think I see at least one person coming already."

Lizzy turned around and followed the tracks. She pursued them about 100 yards to a clump of rocks. The tracks disappeared.

"Damn," Lizzy muttered. It was noonish--the sun was beating down on everything, and she didn't want to go much further without help.

Not to mention, she began to think with growing alarm, who knew who these people were? They could have been Infected; they could have been common bandits. They could have been figments of her imagination.

*This was a stupid thing to do*, she thought.

Still, help was coming, wasn't it? It couldn't hurt to just check a little more. She began to go around the rock when she heard a gunshot behind her.

She whipped around and began to run back to the cactii.

"Polly!?" she yelled, pumping her arms and panting as she ran.

When she got there, Polly was down on the ground, bleeding and still. Olin was standing over her, a smoking pistol in her hand. She looked up at Lizzy with a wild, animal look.

"God, this is fantastic," Olin said, smiling. "Not only do I get to kill the dyke, I get to kill you, too."

*Oh, shit...*

Lizzy felt the blood leave her face. "You're kidding, right?"

"You know," Cynthia continued, tossing her pistol far away, "I'm getting so good at this, I'll just say you resisted arrest and I had to rough you up."

Lizzy's mind raced. She knew some dirty bar tricks, but the phrase "boarding team dyanmo" kept repeating over and over in her mind.

And, didn't Olin mention once about having five older brothers?

"Cynthia," Lizzy said. "C'mon, more are coming..."

"No," she whispered. "They're not. Just me. I told the guards I'd take care of it. I'm here to track you down. Though, I have to tell you I have a 100% mortality rate." She grinned and started to move towards Lizzy.

*I'm fucked,* Lizzy thought. *The hell with it.* She scooped up a handful of sand and threw it in Olin's face.

Olin threw up her hands to block the sand. Some must have gotten in her eyes--she grunted and shook her head. Lizzy began to run.

"Nice try," Lizzy heard Olin say behind her. And then she heard the gunshot.

Lizzy felt a white hot fire tear through her thigh, and she went down with a thud. She struggled back to her feet and tried to keep limping ahead. She heard Cynthia walking up behind her.

*One chance...*Lizzy reached for her taser. From behind, she heard another taser charging. She turned hers on and quickly released it from her holster.

"You have the right to remain silent, Townsend," she heard from behind her. She waited until she swore she could feel Olin's breath on the back of her neck. Then she whipped around and lunged.

Not fast enough. Olin sidestepped her as Lizzy stumbled forward. Olin hit Lizzy in the back of the neck with the taser.

*Oh, hell...*

Lizzy felt the surge and saw her life fade to black.

# •CHAPTER FOURTEEN•

*Commune Ruth*
*Three Days Later*
*1200*

"WHAT THE FUCK WERE YOU THINKING?" Erin screamed. "Goin' out there by yourselves. She could have fuckin' killed you!"

Lizzy was sitting in Erin's office, eyes closed. It was almost a week later, and Lizzy still had a perpetual headache. Her leg pulsed with pain. Once Master Chief said Lizzy could leave her sickbed this morning, Erin wouldn't let her have anything stronger than Ibuprofin.

This put Lizzy in a bad mood. She opened her eyes and glared at Erin. "Maybe if you told people Olin was an assassin with a murder complex, we wouldn't have gone out there, you asshole!" Lizzy snapped.

All and all, though, Lizzy was living a charmed life. Polly had regained consciousness, dragged herself along the desert floor with the shotgun, and shot Olin in the back. Cynthia had lived and was sedated in the clinic. Erin wouldn't tell anyone where Cynthia was going once she was stable enough, but she did assure everyone Olin was going somewhere far from Ruth to answer the charges. Polly hadn't been so lucky—she lost too much blood and had died.

Erin paced back and forth in the tiny office. The stress of the last few days showed on her face. "You didn't need to know she was a Tracker."

"Well, what the fuck, Erin! We didn't need to know she was a fucking psychopath? A Tracker...was she ordered to kill everyone?"

"Fuck, no. I thought...it was suspicious. No one came back alive, but it's not *that* unusual, God...we have one of the lowest mortality rates, Liz, you have no idea."

Lizzy leaned forward in her chair. She winced at the pain in her leg and leaned back again. "You had to think it was more than suspicious, Erin. It isn't great here, but you're fair, and we all know there's nothing out there."

Erin stared at Lizzy. "It's my fault," she finally said. "I saw the pattern, and I should have said something, but...honest to God, she didn't seem that unstable! I never thought she was that homophobic. Shit, I even thought she and McMasters were fucking, everyone did."

Lizzy looked at the floor and shrugged. The pieces fell into place when Olin had shot Polly. Before she died, Polly said Olin had called her a "fuckin' dyke" and that she could "Join her girlfriend and all the other pussy eaters in hell." before she fired her pistol. In addition to Polly's deathbed testimony, Erin and others realized that each of the "disappeared" had been called into Erin's office for a "talking to" at some point for their liaisons with other women. Olin's office was next door, and she could have heard everything.

No one would ever know exactly what happened--Olin denied it all. Three days ago, a few military search parties from Headquarters looked around and found Steph's body behind some rocks about a thousand yards away, with marks of strangulation and assault. If they had the time they might have found more, but Erin figured they had seen enough. She arranged to have the HQ detachment recalled back to their unit and reclassified the "Missing" to "Deceased." Cases closed.

"Tracker duty I had no control over," Erin continued, still pacing. "She reported directly to Headquarters."

Lizzy nodded. *Whatever...*

"What about the tracks?" She wanted to change the subject—this one was making her ill.

Erin paused, and then kept pacing. "Don't know. By the time we got around to them, there wasn't a trace. Sorry, Liz."

"Too bad." Lizzy thought there was more, but Erin wasn't talking. Lizzy wondered why. Frankly, she was getting a little tired of the bullshit and being kept out of the loop. "Who's XPO now?"

Erin stopped pacing, went around her desk, and sat on her chair with a *plop*. "I don't suppose you want it? Technically, you should have had it in the first place, being senior to Olin. You'd have to give up the Lab maintanence, though."

Lizzy shook her head. "Nah, Skids, I like being a grunt." She blinked and looked at Erin, waiting. "Skids" was a despised old nickname from the boat. It was a reference to the one time Lisa forgot to courtesy flush. She wanted to see how Erin would react.

"Aw, fuck off!" Erin growled. "All right, Cage is a SM/5, and we get along. I'll give it to her. You up for travelling tomorrow?"

Lizzy winced at the thought. "My leg still hurts."

Erin held up her hands. "Sorry, Liz. I need you clear for the trip."

Lizzy paused, staring at her. She considered the bumpy roads and potholes of the trip. *Fuckin' bitch...* "Aye, aye, ONIC." Lizzy glared at Erin and pulled herself to her feet. She started to limp out of the room.

"Hey, Liz!" Erin called after her. Lizzy turned around.

"When we get to Headquarters, I'll see what I can do to get you some codeine or somethin'. We'll have a million other Sensors. No need for you to be workin'."

Lizzy nodded. "Thanks, Erin."

# ·CHAPTER FIFTEEN·

*District Headquarters*
*The Next Day*
*1500*

"Thank God for AC," Lizzy commented, climbing out of the van in the HQ parking lot and wincing as the desert heat hit her in the face. The van was fully equipped, and was only used for special occasions. Specifically, Erin's rare trips out of Ruth.

"I need to get AC in my office," Erin said, squinting in the sun. "When does rank get to have its privilages, anyway?"

"Are you fuckin' nuts?" Lizzy said, grouchy and perhaps not as respectful as she should be. "We'd have to keep two generators going just for that."

Erin gave Lizzy a sidelong glance. "Fuck off," she muttered. "You know, you're a real pain in the ass."

Lizzy's lips smiled sweetly; her eyes didn't smile. Her leg was throbbing. Erin could take her air conditioners and shove them up her pained ass. And she still wasn't sure what do to about Erin and the Tracker situation.

Headquarters was located at an abandoned office complex; after Infusion, when the government decided to move in somewhere, it was quite convenient--the soldiers just had to remove the body pieces and make any modifications they wanted.

Like the Lab, HQ was outfitted with an indoor swimming pool and a full fitness center. In addition, they had a physical therapy department, a full ER and trauma center, operating rooms, and a dental clinic. A small airport was located out back. Lizzy wondered how often all that stuff was really used.

She had been there twice before--they had wanted vials of blood for research--but she always dreaded coming there. As she approached the gate, a wave of nausea washed over her. She fumbled for her anacid as they slowly walked toward the entrance.

"You OK?" Erin asked, touching her shoulder.

"This place has a lot of Infected materials," Lizzy answered, picking out two tablets and shoving them in her mouth. "It's like being really, really seasick."

Erin nodded. "You going to make it?"

"Mmmm. The codeine or whatever would help. Hold on." Lizzy limped over to a nearby bush. She retched and vomited behind it. When she had emptied her stomach, she turned and wobbled back to the path.

"Just like seasickness: you puke, you feel better," Lizzy commented, wiping her mouth with the palm of her hand and her hand on her pants.

They arrived at the front gate, where two Marines in BDUs stood watch. One of them, a large African-American built like a tree trunk, walked to the fence with a clipboard. Erin approached him and showed him her ID card.

"Names?"

"BM2/8 Erin Phillips, USCG. DC2/7 Elizabeth Townsend, USCG."

The Marine checked the list. "Yes. Where are you from?"

"Commune Outpost Ruth."

"Coordinates?"

"Second star on the right, fly 'till morning."

Behind Erin, Lizzy smiled to herself. She wondered how many grunts recognized the "Peter Pan" reference.

"Yes. You may pass."

The gate *clicked*, the wheels began to turn, and the fence slid opened. As Lizzy passed, she noticed The Tree Trunk looked a little green and was swallowing a lot.

She made eye contact and asked, "Sensor?"

The man nodded and swallowed.

"What level?"

The man grimaced slightly. "Around Level 2."

"Damn," Lizzy said as she glanced at the complex. Her stomach growled. "How do you take it? I had to puke already, and I just got here."

The Marine glanced down the path. More people were coming. "They have new meds that help a little. They should talk about them at the meeting. Excuse me." He turned around and approached the gate again.

Lizzy hobbled up to Erin on the path. "They have Infected blockers now," Lizzy told her.

Erin gave her a sidelong look and scrunched her face up into a question. "Then, what's the point of being a Sensor?"

"Well, not totally. That guy back there is Level 2, and he's holding his own."

"Mm," Erin grunted. They walked on.

◆　◆　◆　◆

*District Headquarters*
*Room 113*
*The Next Day*
*0800*

Lizzy had no idea there were so many Outposts in this area. There were a good eighty people in the Conference Room, chit-chatting about gardens and children and weather. She saw The Tree Trunk Marine with all the men in the room. The thirty of them were huddled together, an oasis of testosterone in a foreign, mostly XX-chromosome land.

The room looked like any other large conference room in pre-Infusion America: white walls, blue pile carpeting, generic blended pictures on the wall, and blue stacking chairs arranged in rows facing a white screen in the front of the room. Lizzy looked around, trying to find someone she knew.

Jessica was up front, writing on a dry-erase board. Lizzy crossed the room and limped up to the front.

"Hi!"

Jessica turned around. "Hey, yourself! How's the leg?"

Lizzy was a little surprised. "They let you read the report? I didn't think it'd get to the lab."

"Yes," Jessica replied. "BM2 Olin will be coming to the lab for a couple

80

of days, and she's in my charge."

"Fuck. You know how dangerous she is, right?"

"Yes. All the proper precautions will be taken."

Lizzy nodded. "The leg's fine, thanks. They let me have some narcs this morning and I'm flying high. How's Mike?"

Jessica smiled. "He acted like he was sick, as usual." Mike always managed to spontaneously contract double pneumonia when Jessica told him she had a trip coming up. "He's working on something, though. That'll keep him occupied."

"How's Bea?"

"Fine, the last time I talked to her. She and Samuel are a thing now."

"This week," Lizzy corrected.

"This week," Jessica agreed, smirking.

Lizzy grinned. "Hey, can I help you set up?"

"Nah, I'm almost done. We'll be starting soon." She paused and looked to the back. "Actually, can you get me an apple cider? Can your leg handle it?"

"No problem." Lizzy turned and hobbled to the back of the room.

The spread was reminiscent of ye olde office meetings gone by. Arranged on the table were doughnuts and streudels, albeit made in the kitchens rather than the supermarket bakery. In addition to the traditional coffee, tea, and milk, they offered apple and pear ciders, and apricot and peach juices in season. Colas and other soft drinks had disappeared soon after modern civilization fell, though occasionally someone would make some homemade batches with yeast. It was the same there as at the Outposts and Laboratories--there was fresh food and drink everywhere, and no one knew how. The Garden of Eden could be next door, and no one would have ever dared ask how it got there.

It amused Lizzy to watch about half the people in the room eating and drinking, while the other half was noticeably avoiding even looking at food; she was glad for the bottle of narcotics she got from the Doc this morning. As Lizzy poured apple cider into a tumbler, she heard a voice behind her.

"How are you still standing?"

Lizzy turned around. A dark-haired, dark-eyed, middle-aged woman in an ivory suit was studying her.

"Excuse me?" Lizzy asked.

"You've got to be the strongest Sensor I've ever felt. Why aren't you on the floor?" She sipped her cup of tea.

Lizzy turned slightly and poured herself a cup of orange juice. "I'm on painkillers--I got shot in the leg."

"Wow--that's too bad. How did it happen?" she asked, looking interested.

"Excuse me, but...how do you know that I'm a Sensor?" Lizzy asked, for some reason wanting to change the subject in a hurry.

"That's my gift," the woman answered, smiling. "I can't sense demons, but I can sense Sensors. My name's Abby." She held out her hand. It had a lot of jewelry on it. Her nails were carefully manicured and painted ivory to match her suit.

Lizzy took her hand. "Lizzy Townsend."

Abby squeezed her hand. "Well, now, that explains it. No wonder they were after you at that laboratory."

Lizzy glanced to see if anyone was eavesdropping. "Do you work for Headquarters?" She pulled her hand back as quickly as manners would allow. She couldn't help it--there was something about Abby that was...well...greasy.

"Mmmm...not exactly. I'm what you might call a consultant. As far as I know, I'm the only one who can do what I do." She turned and took Lizzy's arm. "I'm so glad I met you. Shall we take our seats?"

"Sure. Just need to deliver this, and I'll be right with you." She pulled her arm from Abby's grasp and went to the front.

"Jessica," Lizzy said quietly, smiling as she handed the cup to her. "Casually, look two o' clock at the woman in the ivory suit, jet black hair."

Jessica pretended to cough and glanced at Abby. "Yeah?"

"Do you know her?"

"No, why?"

Lizzy kept smiling and playfully punched Jessica's arm. "Her name's Abby. She says she can sense Sensors."

Jessica reached over and tousled Lizzy's hair and smiled back. Her eyes, however, held her surprise. "No, never heard of her."

"OK." She waved at Jessica and took her seat next to Abby.

Abby leaned over and whispered, "Would you introduce me to Jessica Donovan later? She's done some very interesting papers on demon behavior. I'd forgotten you two know each other."

Lizzy showed teeth and said, "Of course." Lizzy was feeling nauseous again, but this time demon materials had nothing to do with it. Abby's syrupy sweetness was washing over her in cloying waves.

Thank God that in the front of the room, Jessica approached the podium and turned the microphone on. She announced, "We're ready to begin. If you would, please take your seats."

◆　◆　◆　◆

*1208*

"I don't know why they make me go to these things," Erin complained, twirling spaghetti with her fork. "It's all your shit."

"This would be the 'rank has its privileges' part," Lizzy returned, smirking. "Besides, it's all for survival, y'know. It's important."

They were in the center of Headquarter's huge cafeteria. *The morning* was *boring*, Lizzy admitted to herself. It was mostly review about stuff she already knew, but they did go over the lab incident. Abby had leaned over and winked at Lizzy when the speaker mentioned there was an unnamed maintanence person involved. Lizzy had to concentrate not to throw up on her.

The story hadn't been public knowledge, judging by people's reactions to the story. The majority of the people's faces were drained of color throughout the report.

About 1130 they broke for lunch, and Lizzy decided to eat with Erin. She figured Erin wasn't important enough for Abby's time, and perhaps she would eat elsewhere.

Sure enough, Abby planted herself next to Jessica and some scientists. Jessica seemed to be enjoying herself--a rescue wasn't required. Lizzy turned back to Erin. "Find anyone you know here?"

It straddled the "don't ask" boundary, but Erin answered her. "Yeah," she began, and started pointing around the room.

"OK, over there is Doug McClellon, and he's head of Outpost Matthew. Wouldn't wanna be him. Over there," she pointed to a Latino woman in a Navy uniform, "is Marlene Santigo. She's really nice. I forgot where I met her..."

It turned out Erin knew quite a few people. Lizzy sat amused: *just like the old Erin of the ship...always connected.* Finally Erin took one last sweeping glance and said, "...and that's it. How about you?"

Lizzy looked around. "The only people I know are Jessica Donovan, over there in the pink and white, and Abby-somebody, in the ivory suit."

Erin squinted at the table. "She looks familiar..."

"Really?" Lizzy asked. "She's really good at name-dropping. Some consultant for the government. Says she can sense Sensors."

"No shit?"

"No shit."

"Hmmm..." Erin said. "I've never met her, I don't think, but I've seen her before." She turned back around and chewed on her piece of bread, absorbed in thought.

The rest of the lunch was eaten in silence. While Erin went through her mental filing cabinet, Lizzy concentrated on the next table, sending out mental feelers, trying to see if she could sense Abby. The narcotic was starting to wear off--she was already in danger of losing her lunch--but Abby was an enigma. She felt like any other normal person.

Finally, Erin and Lizzy stood up and headed for the galley. "Hell, I dunno," Erin finally concluded. "Hey, are you going to the pool party tonight?"

Lizzy frowned. "Wasn't planning on it. Never even heard about it."

"The flyer was on the refreshment table. About 1800, after dinner. Did you bring your suit?"

Lizzy shook her head. "No, but I wouldn't mind hanging out."

"Neither did I. It would have been nice if they fuckin' told us ahead of time about it."

Erin paused and got another thoughtful look. "They're really getting chummy, y'know? They've never done this before..."

"Maybe it's a morale thing. We did get bad news today. Besides, when was the last time you were in a pool?"

"Yeah," Erin agreed, dropping the topic. They dumped their trays and went back to the conference room.

♦ ♦ ♦ ♦

*Room 213*
*1703*

Erin turned on the tub faucet, relishing the steaming hot water coming from the tap. The solar panels did a decent job of heating the shower water back at Ruth, but nothing compared to a hotel-sized water heater set at 120 degrees. Erin undressed and tied her hair up. She stepped into the tub and sank into the water.

As she lay among the bubbles, she suddenly felt--strange. She sat up...concern quickly gave way to panic. She started to get up, but her arms slipped and she splashed back down. The room began to spin.

*Something...her feel fuzzy, want to...a flash...*

*...no...*

Erin's frame sat up and looked down at the body.

*Good one,* the first said.

*Yes,* the second one answered. *Bring the others.*

*Pool Room*
*1745*

PFC Myers grumbled as she punched the double door opened. A rush of warm, damp air hit her face as she went into the pool area.

She was sent to check the chemicals for tonight's pool party. She *hated* parties hosted by Headquarters--all the enlisted broke their backs and did bullshit work so officers could shmooze. Meanwhile, not even a "thank you" from any of them...

The sun was going down, but there was enough natural light coming through the row of windows near the ceiling that she didn't bother with the overhead lights. Myers was past the pool and almost to the treatment room when she noticed that not only was the room unlocked, it was slightly ajar.

*Fuckin' Turner,* She thought. *I woulda gotten blamed...*

She pushed the door opened and walked inside. She felt along the wall next to her for the switch.

Then she hit something sharp with her fingers.

"OUCH!" she yelped.

She saw a flash of light...

# ·CHAPTER SIXTEEN·

The pool party was a raving success. The music was blaring, the punch had been spiked and was flowing, and the few that were dancing on the mosaic tile floor got crazier and crazier with every song. Most of the people were in the pool trying to play volleyball through their alcoholic haze. A lifeguard had been assigned and was on the tower above, sober and watching carefully.

Lizzy sat with Jessica, holding a cup of water. One whiff of the punch told her what was in it, and she didn't want to mix punch with the pills and end up on her ass. They sat on two beach chairs, talking while watching the debauchery.

"So Mike," Jessica was yelling over the base and percussion, "takes a beer bong, hacks off the ends, and with surgical precision performs a tracheostomy on the patio table."

Lizzy's eyes widened in astonishment.

"Later, when his father drilled him about how he had learned to do all that, Mike admitted he had snuck his dad's old textbooks and read them during class."

"And he was only 14?"

"Yup. It was in all the papers. His Dad didn't even ask why a bong was at the party--he knew Mike too well to ask. But it was the first time Mike's dad thought he was worth something."

"Damn," Lizzy said. "That's harsh. Maybe his dad shouldn't have been so hard on him, y'know?" She paused and looked up.

"Well, he was a 'C' student, and all of his brothers and sisters were on the honor roll and...Lizzy? What's wrong?"

Lizzy was on her feet, looking at the far double doors. She felt something...from her nightmares. Back at Newport--she remembered the feeling.

*Oh, God...not again...*

"Something's coming," she said.

Above them, as The Kingsman strummed the opening to "Louie, Louie," Jessica paled.

Two or three people had now also stopped to look at the door. One even began to scream, but the music drowned her out. The rest of the group played on, too drunk or oblivious to notice.

Neither woman could move; their bodies refused to work.

Finally, Jessica looked at Lizzy. She bent down and spoke next Lizzy's ear.

"I'm sorry. But, I think it will be OK."

Lizzy began to ask what she meant by that, but Jessica rose and stood, never taking her eyes off the door.

In the same moment Jessica managed to get to her feet, PFC Myers hurtled through the door. The knife in her hand flashed in the overhead lights. Without a sound or any wasted movement, she jumped in the pool. The knife began to shine with a rhythm of white flashes as Myers cut and slashed and hacked.

The water around her began to turn red. Her victims were strangely calm.

A second later, Erin entered the other set of doors. Lizzy almost yelled to warn her, but then she felt the overwhelming desire to vomit. Even doped up Lizzy could feel the demons inside her friend. There were several in Erin, she knew--she felt them. Erin was cut in several places, and blood was oozing all over her body. Erin charged like a bull towards a group of people standing by the water's edge, dazed by the bloodshed. She pushed, and the people fell into the water.

Then Lizzy was temporarily distracted by noise and movement through the double-door windows leading to the passageway. To her horror, Lizzy saw steel shutters slam down, blocking the way out right past the doors. The shutters looked solid enough to hold them, and Lizzy was sure they went from ceiling to floor. They were trapped.

Lizzy looked poolside again. Erin was moving.

"Erin!" Lizzy cried as she saw her friend throw herself into the water. As Erin thrashed around, she could almost see the demons spreading throughout the rest of the people in the pool. It would be over in moments.

She grabbed Jessica's hand and fell to her knees beside the pool. She had no idea if she could do it, but she had to try.

"Pray," she yelled to Jessica over the screaming and the pain in her leg.

Lizzy plunged her hand into the water and began to search within herself for that feeling she had when she believed in God, when the Power of Christ seemed so strong, so alive, so right...

In that moment Lizzy felt something, and she focused on it, thinking about how it felt, the balance, the rightness, the rightness of God's creation, pure...

Without warning she saw in her mind the image of the geyser of white energy and power. It was rising from deep within her before she felt its presence. It was brilliant and solid. When it came, it exploded throughout her being and channeled down her arm and out her hand, like lightning through steel, finding the path of least resistance. She heard herself gasp. When her eyes were closed, she saw nothing but light. She opened her eyes and looked down.

The pool was beginning to boil.

Lizzy concentrated on the Rightousness while Infused screamed and were scalded. Some only felt pain for a few seconds, and then were exorcized and left limp and drained. Others that were host to two or more and shook, boiling and smoking, within the water.

Erin had submerged when the water bubbled, and now Lizzy saw her surface. All of her hair was gone; her scalp was melting, revealing the white skull beneath.

Lizzy wanted to stop, but found she couldn't; it was like trying to stop a tidal wave. She knew somehow that the power wouldn't go until all the demons were gone. She started to pull away, but then considered Erin would want release, one way or another--she kept going. With each second, the power became easier to manage. It was no longer overwhelming--it flowed easier, even though it was still consuming.

"Erin," she whispered, feeling her friend's life ebbing faster than the possession. "Please, hang on."

Around her, people at the edge of the pool were beginning to snap back into reality. The lifeguard climbed down from the tower and grabbed the lifehook. He bent down and skimmed the water towards Lisa's body, which was now sitting like a buoy, bobbing up and down with the waves. What was left of Erin's face and skin from the waist up was turning ash grey. People outside the pool began bending down and dragging the cleansed out.

The demons were almost gone. They were slipping away.

*Just a few more seconds...yes.*  And then they were gone.

And then as quickly as it had come, the power left.  The water went calm. The lifeguard got a hold of Erin's body and pulled.

The hook ripped Erin in half as if she were made of wet toilet paper. Everyone went silent as the halves began to float away from each other.

Erin was gone.  Her body now disintergrated into the pool, bits of burnt fat and skin like chopped winter leaves spread on top of the water.

Lizzy slumped to the tiled floor, still clutching Jessica's hand.  She began to cry.  Jessica could only sit next to her and let Lizzy keep clutching her hand.

Once the crisis had ended the doors were raised, and a squad of soldiers armed and dressed in riot gear flooded both entrances.

"NOBODY MOVE!" one of them yelled.  Everyone froze.

"Get the wounded!  The rest, file out!" the same soldier shouted.  The men dispersed, and order began to return.  Jessica withdrew her hand, stood, and then quietly left the room.

A man from the conference walked up to Lizzy.  He put a comforting hand on her shoulder.  She looked up into his face.

"So," he said, nodding towards the pool.  He was smiling slightly.  "Is this now holy water?"

Lizzy somehow instantly knew the answer.

"No," she told him.  "Once it takes a life, and there is no replenishment, it is tainted.  It is only dirty filth."  No one had told her that--somehow, she just knew.

The man looked down and wrinkled his nose at the pieces of her dead friend.  "Then, what good is it?" he said in disgust, as he dropped his hand and walked away.

*Yeah,* Lizzy thought, looking around at the carnage, *What good is it?*

# ◆CHAPTER SEVENTEEN◆

*District Headquarters*
*The Next Day*
*1000*

Lizzy had been woken up two hours earlier and informed Abigail Burgess wanted to see her in Room 102 at 1000.

After the security watchstander had left, Lizzy rolled over and went back to sleep. Around 0955, she woke up, got out of bed, and threw on a pair of coveralls and boondockers. As an afterthought, she packed her bag, strapped her tazer onto her thigh, and pocketed her bottle of painkillers and the van keys--as soon as this little meeting was over, she was heading back to Ruth. As she crossed the room to fetch her cover, she noticed the pain in her leg was gone. She was queasy--it had been last night since she took her meds--but her leg was fine now.

*Groovy perk to boiling people alive...*

She pulled her cover down over her unwashed hair and walked to Room 102.

The door was opened, and Abby was at her desk, furiously typing on her laptop. She never looked up.

"Lizzy?" she called. "I know you're there. Please come in."

Lizzy fumed to herself and walked into the room. Ms. Burgess had an art deco decor, with lots of matte metals and triangles and distinct lines.

*Not bad,* Lizzy thought, taking it all in. *Wonder how many homes of dead people she had to rummage through to get this spread?*

"Please sit down," Abby said, interrupting her thoughts. Lizzy went to the closest chair and slumped down into it.

Abby gave her a disapproving glance, and then put the shiny/happy mask on again. "Quite a day yesterday, wasn't it, Lizzy?"

Lizzy stared at her incredulously.

Seeing she wasn't going to get a reply, Abby babbled on. "Yes, it was too bad about Erin Phillips. You two were friends, weren't you?"

Silence.

"Well, it was quite amazing what you did. You know," Abby leaned in closer, "you were never really tested at Newport for holy water. I checked. You passed out before the test, and you would never try after that. I think I would have pushed you a little harder, but it was a turbulent time, and you were such a novelty. I can see how they would go easy on you.

"We never would have known," she continued, "if this hadn't had happened. That would have been tragic, that talent never brought to light, don't you think?" She looked into Lizzy's eyes and smiled.

Lizzy felt her eyes involuntarily widen, and she didn't say anything for a long minute. She broke her gaze and stared at the back of Abby's laptop for several seconds. Then, when Lizzy could speak, her voice was low.

"You can't tell me, that all of those people...all those Sensors...Erin...was a setup?"

"Well, not exactly. We had hoped someone would step up to the plate, you might say, but we weren't positive it was going to be you."

"How..." She paused. She considered.

*Do I really want to know this?*

*Fuck it.* She took a breath.

"How did you know they would attack?"

"Oh, we didn't, but when would they get a better opportunity to get rid of some Sensors? It was a calculated risk, you see? At best, it would be a great party where nothing bad happened. At worst, they Infect you all. But somewhere in the middle--well, it was truly amazing, really." She smiled at Lizzy.

*This woman is either insane or evil*, Lizzy thought. She pondered if she could commit cold-blooded murder, if it came to it. The way this conversation was going, it might have to.

*But maybe you won't have to, Lizzy, so play along...*

"So, what happens now?" she asked Abby.

Abby arranged herself in a classic therapist position--back straight, elbows on armrest, fingers mingled at nose level, legs crossed--and pretended to consider Lizzy for a few moments.

*Y'know, Bitch, I can play this game, too,* Lizzy thought, not breaking her stare. She figured Abby wasn't used to people being rude to her.

Finally Abby turned away and stared at a point on the wall. She cleared her throat. "You'll be staying here. There are several tests we need to do--brain activity during exorcism, your chemical makeup, what you do to the possessed bodies--my goodness, months of tests."

Lizzy could feel a nugget of panic starting to form in the pit of her stomach. "Are you out of your fucking mind? You just can't slaughter people like lab rats. And if you think I'll be a part of your fucking experiments..."

Abby-the-Happy suddenly turned off like a switch and was immediately replaced by Abby-the-Pissed.

"Maybe you missed something," she hissed, interrupting, "but humans are losing this war. Sacrifices have to be made, which means I don't give a shit about what you think, or how many Infected you kill, or how much you miss your dead husband or your little lab friends. You're an amateur white-trash nothing with a gift that was wasted on you, and YOU WILL DO AS I SAY! " she finished, shrieking.

At the word "missed," Lizzy had turned on her taser. Abby's shouting had drowned out the hum of its charging.

*She has a point about it being a war,* Lizzy admitted to herself, but something told her she wouldn't live long here. Not under this psycho's charge. And, there was no way in hell she could watch another body fall apart like that.

Six years ago, someone yelling at her like this would have crushed her. Now, it just made her mad. She quickly realized her life wasn't worth shit anymore. She made a choice, and she formed a plan. She had never done anything as ballsy as what she was about to do in her life, but Lizzy knew it was time to leave.

She had finally arrived at her own Triggering Event.

Around the "not giving a shit" part she slipped the taser out of the holster and palmed it. She kept her eyes locked on Abby's as she stood up and leaned over the desk so she was almost nose-to-nose with screaming woman. Abby was around the "white-trash nothing" highlight at this point, so she was too absorbed to noticed the close proximity. Or perhaps she didn't care. Lizzy shifted her arm so the taser was behind the opened laptop, out of sight.

When Abby finally finished and Lizzy answered her, it was simple, slow, and quiet.

"I'd rather die in the Wilderness. Fuck you."

Lizzy jerked upward and jabbed Abby in the chest with the taser. There was a blue and white flash, a puff of smoke, and Abby fell in her chair, eyes wide opened, twitching.

Lizzy whipped around to see if anyone noticed in the doorway.

*No...lucky.* They must be used to Abby's temper tantrums.

She quickly crossed the room and shut the door. She went back to Abby and checked her neck for a pulse. There was one, but it was thready.

Now Lizzy's morality slammed into her. She knew she should kill Abby outright, but she just wasn't ready to do it. However, she did need a way to cover this up until she could leave. Her mind sped through scenarios. Finally, she settled on one thought:

*A suicide.*

Lizzy couldn't murder anyone, she was pretty sure, but she could live with playing Russian roulette with this murdering bitch and letting fate decide. She emptied her bottle of narcotics into her palm and placed the pills between Abby's cheeks and gums. If it didn't kill her, it would at least knock her out for a very long time.

She grabbed a mug on Abby's desk and poured the cold coffee over Abby's shirt, hiding the taser burn if someone didn't look too hard. She pulled the chair back and pushed Abby to the floor, then halfway into the kneehole. Lizzy stepped back and leaned against the far door. From the doorway, no one could see her. If she was found, they may think at first she had a heart attack. Later, when they found the pills, a suicide. It might buy her time.

*Either way, I'm committed now. I have to get out.*

# ·CHAPTER EIGHTEEN·

*District Headquarters*
*Room 102*
*1030*

Lizzy's mind raced. She couldn't go back to the commune--no help there. The only place she could go was the lab. She figured she had at most six hours before Abby woke up, if the overdose didn't kill her. Or sooner, if she had a meeting or something.

The radio room was in the basement. She had to disable the radios, get to the van, drive to the lab, then pray to God (she might actually do that now) that someone could help her.

Then it hit her: the antenna. If she could cut the wires to the antenna, no one would nessessarily notice, or would check everything else first. She headed for the nearest stairwell and went up.

*1045*

Dr. Egan knocked on the door to Room 102. "Abby?' he called. Nothing. He cracked the door opened and glanced inside. No one was there. They had a meeting at 1100, and she had asked him to stop by first.

*Oh, well*, he thought. He shut the door and continued to the meeting.

*1049*

Lizzy hunched over the doorknob, multi-tool in hand. The door was locked, but the guys who installed the doorknob had installed it backwards. She could remove it.

"Sometimes it's good to be a DC," she muttered. She popped the knob off. When all that was left was a hole in the door and the latch, she stopped and considered the door.

Any wires? Alarms? She didn't see any. She pulled the latch in, pushed the door out an inch and checked again.

There...in the door jamb...half of a spring-loaded button that would pop out when the door was opened. It might have been more effective on the hinge side, but it was still very, very clever.

*You're very sly, but so am I*, Lizzy thought, smirking. She pulled the door shut and inserted the cylinder to keep it closed. She dusted herself off and bent down. With a jerking motion, she ripped the pant hem of her coveralls. Dragging her ripped pant leg behind her, she climbed down the ladder and went to find the nearest maintenance guy. She had to borrow some duct tape to fix her pant hem.

*1115*

*OK, that took way too long*, she thought to herself, walking back to the door. She pulled the duct tape off her coveralls and removed the cylinder. She moved the door out an inch and caught the button with her thumb. A few moments

91

later, Lizzy stepped out on the roof in peace and quiet.

She crouched low and ran towards the antenna. She hoped to God there wasn't any current going through the wires, or she was fucked.

Well…she supposed?

*Isn't an antenna just for amplification?*

She wasn't sure. The only tool she had was her pocket tool, and it was steel--that probably wasn't good. There were rubber gloves on the wall, but who knew how much that would help?

The antenna was a huge steel tower. The two cables that went down below were each an inch thick. Sighing, Lizzy picked out the saw tool and got on her knees. She slipped the gloves on her hands and got to work on the cable casings. What she would give for bolt cutters...

*1120*

The weekly research meeting had convened, but hadn't started yet. The Special Liaison of Sensor Research and Development was missing.

"I checked her office, Don, but she wasn't there," Dr. Egan said.

Dr. Hart picked up the phone reciever next to him and punched four numbers on the keypad. After a few moments he pressed the button to hang up and punched the button to page her over the PA system. When she didn't respond, Dr. Hart frowned.

"Well, let's start the meeting. I'm sure she'll be here when she can."

*Maybe she's on the bottle again*, Dr. Egan thought. She'd been sober for a while, though, and even drunk she had never missed a meeting...

*1129*

Fingers and hands sore, Lizzy was down to the wires. She put the now-dulled saw away and began cutting the twisted copper strands, a few at a time.

*1130*

"Shit!" RM2 Candy exclaimed, turning down the radio speakers. "Where did all this static come from? Damn, that's loud!"

"Maybe a storm's coming. Or a solar flare?" RM1 Beckerman considered. "It'll pass. Wait a few minutes, then call Matthew. They'll be OK with us being late."

*1135*

Lizzy completed the last cut. Weary, she slowly stood, wincing at the pain in her knees. She turned and walked towards the door. The battle was half over.

*1135 and 30 seconds*

"Outpost Matthew, Outpost Matthew, Outpost Matthew, this is HQ, this is HQ, are you there, over?" Pause. Nothing. Candy tried again.

"Matthew, do you copy, over?" Static.

"That's weird," Beckerman commented. "The interference stopped. Should be OK now."

"Could be a storm still," Candy replied. "I'll wait ten minutes and try again."

Lizzy was getting hungry. She quickly reattached the cylinder and knob and shut the door. She dusted herself off and headed to the cafeteria. Lunch was almost over, but she could grab an apple before hitting the road.

*1138*

"Commune Numbers, Commune Numbers, Commune Numbers, this is HQ, this is HQ, do you copy, over?"

Releasing the button, Candy turned to Beckerman. "All these posts can't be in a storm. We're not receiving."

Beckerman leaned against the counter and began to troubleshoot in his mind. "All right," he sighed. "Check the breakers first. Maybe we'll be lucky and one just tripped."

*1140*

The meeting was over, and Abby still hadn't shown up. Dr. Egan walked down the hallway and knocked on the door again. "Abby?" he called. He opened the door and stepped into the office. Abby was no where to be seen. Crossing the room, he went around the desk to check her laptop and appointment book.

That's when he noticed the smell. He looked down and saw Abigail on the floor--limp, drooling, and laying in her own excrement. He also noticed a half-dissolved pink tablet lying on the floor.

"Oh, my God," he whispered. He punched the PA button on the phone and screamed, "NOW CODE BLUE! CODE BLUE IN ROOM 102!"

*1141*

Lizzy heard the announcement in the cafeteria. *Time to go.* She made a beeline for the exit, two bananas in hand.
*1143*

The trauma team poured into Abby's office, along with a gurney and a crash cart. They quickly rolled her onto a blanket and hoisted her onto the gurney.

Dr. Egan held up the pill. "I found this..."

"What the hell is this?" a nurse interrupted, eyeing the large black spot on Abby's shirt.

"Don't know," an attendant replied as he hooked up monitors. "BP 60 over 40, pulse 50 and thready. Breathing labored."

"Check her mouth for more pills before you insert the airway," the nurse instructed, tying off Abby's arm and patting for a vein.

The attendant opened Abby's mouth and looked. "I don't see anything."

"Hand me the scissors," the doctor said. He quickly snipped the shirt off. "Jesus," he breathed. "She's burned."

Everyone paused and looked at Abby's chest. Two black prong marks were clearly on her skin.

"Damn," the nurse said. "Taser."

Dr. Egan took one look, picked up the phone, and punched in some numbers as the rest kept working. "Is this the front gate? Lock it down! Let no one leave!"

*1150*

Lizzy saw the commotion at the front gate and knew her luck had run out. The guards were armed and alert. She walked to the gate. The Tree Trunk met her halfway and racked the slide.

"You can't leave," the Tree Trunk said. "We're locked down, something's wrong. Was it you?"

Lizzy studied the Tree Trunk. She saw from his shirt his name was Miller. He was a Sensor, and was in pain. Maybe she could level with him. It was her last playing card, anyway.

"Remember the pool last night?" she asked. Miller nodded. "They set that up. They want me to do that again. I have to go."

Miller the Tree Trunk looked torn. He looked at her, looked at the gate, looked around, and then looked at her again.

Then his face smoothed into calm. He had made his choice. "You saved our lives. They had us. Even if you're lying, I owe you one. Struggle with me, then take my gun away."

She put her hands on the gun. After a couple of seconds of twisting, she wrenched the gun away. Miller put up his hands and walked to the gate. Lizzy followed, pointing the gun at his back.

As they approached, Miller's partner looked on in amazement. "How...?"

"Sorry, Johnny," Miller said, shrugging. "She just overpowered me."

Johnny's eyes went from the 6'4" male marine to the 5'4" female coastie.

"You've gotta be shittin' me," Johnny said.

"Look," Lizzy snapped, gesturing with the rifle. "Step away from the rifle and open the gate."

Johnny did as he was told. Lizzy walked over and shouldered the other M-16. "Over there," she instructed. They moved away from the shack and stood on the lawn. She went into the enclosure and pulled the reciever from the phone.

*Now what?* She didn't want to shoot the guards.

Miller, in the meantime, had been quickly telling Johnny who she was.

"So, what, now we're supposed to just let her go?" Johnny asked when Miller had finished. "That's bullshit! I'm not gonna get booked for her..."

"Look, man," Miller said. "You weren't there. They locked us in. I don't think they know what she's capable of, but I *do* know with her around our lives aren't worth shit! Play along; I'll take the blame."

Johnny glared at Miller, and then nodded. "All right."

When Lizzy came out of the shack, out of ideas, Johnny walked past her and opened the gate.

"Just go," he said, frowning. "I guess you're just one tough bitch."

Lizzy smiled and sprinted through the gates. She raced to the van, oblivious to the gate guards behind her, quickly trying to find places to handcuff themselves and throwing their keys into the grass.

# ·CHAPTER NINETEEN·

Abby was out of the Room 102 and was being wheeled to the ER when Dr. Egan finally remembered to look on her laptop. He saw Abby had been writing a report about Elizabeth Townsend.

He groaned. "I'm a goddamned idiot." He tried to patch through the front gate, but this time there was no answer.

Dr. Egan began to panic. He punched the quick dial button for Security.


1215

"WHAT DO YOU MEAN SHE JUST OVERPOWERED YOU, MILLER?" the captain screamed.


1230

"She has a thirty minute head-start," the team leader said into his commco, trying to talk and drive at the same time. "We're going to the Alpha lab. Charlie, y'all are going to Ruth. Keep in contact. Out."


1237

"WHAT DO YOU MEAN IT'S BROKEN?" Dr. Hart yelled.

Beckerman stood his ground. "Look, we're doing everything we can, sir. We've been tracing cables, and there's someone on the roof now."

Beckerman's commco crackled. "RM1, this is RM2."

Beckerman took the radio out of his belt. "Yeah."

"The wiring's been cut. Real butcher job, too. We're going to have to lay new stuff."

Beckerman turned a slight shade of pale. "She was on the roof?"

"Looks that way."

"Jesus...she's damn lucky we didn't transmit. She'd 've been fried." He sighed. "All right, I'll be there to help in a minute. RM1 out." Beckerman clipped his commco back in his belt.

"Pain-in-the-ass bitch," he muttered to himself. Then he turned to Dr. Hart. "Don't expect communications for at least four hours."

"That's not acceptable!" Dr. Hart replied, agast. "She tried to kill someone! We have to warn people!"

"I'm sorry, sir." RM1 replied. "We have to replace and rerun all the cables. We're cold, dark, and quiet."

95

*1245*

Lizzy parked the van in front of the laboratory. She made her way to Larry, hoping the question would be easy this time.

*1250*

*Security at these bases is pathetic,* Lizzy thought as she walked briskly through the double doors. *Same damn answer...*"fly 'till morning..."

*1251*

Larry picked up his shack phone and called his assistant.

"Would you cover me for a minute? Lizzy parked in a bad spot, and I have to move the van. Thanks, Rick."

*1252*

Lizzy had carefully considered who to ask for help. She settled on Bea: she still might be feeling guilty about the birthday present, she had connections, and she was ballsier than Mike. For all of Mike's bluster, at heart he was a Chickenshit when it came to authority.

Also Jessica, Mike's wife, somehow knew the attack was coming. It physically hurt to consider the possible conclusions she could make with that fact; Lizzy would have to ponder that another time.

She went to Lab 1 and walked in. The lab was empty. Lizzy went to the back and found Bea sitting in her office, writing.

"Hey!" Bea yelled, big grin on her face. She stood up and started to walk around the desk. "Didn't know you were coming today. I could have told Samuel, could have had lunch..."

Then Bea really looked at Lizzy. Dirty, panicked, and pale. "What happened?"

Lizzy shut the door behind her. "I'm in big trouble," Lizzy began. "They're trying to kill me, and I need a way out."

Bea leaned forward. "Who's trying to kill you?"

Lizzy huffed. "Look, you really don't want to know, 'cause they'll ask later, OK? Do you know anyone who can get me to safety?"

Bea considered this for several moments. Finally, she took a post-it pad off the desk and scribbled on it. She ripped the note off and walked over to Lizzy. She put her arms around her. "I'm really going to miss you," she said, hugging Lizzy tight. She handed Lizzy the note.

"Take this to Dr. Goddard. Make sure you're alone. And good luck."

Bea took Lizzy by the elbow, opened the door, gently pushed her out, and then closed the door behind her.

Lizzy looked down at the note. It read:

*Lizzy is my friend. She may have my seat at poker tonight. Bea.*

Lizzy had no idea where Dr. Goddard was. She had spoken to her maybe twice in five years. Dr. Goddard liked to keep to herself, at least around Lizzy. Just for a starting place, she checked Goddard's office.

Sure enough, the pure white lab coat was on the peg next to her desk. Goddard was at her computer.

"Yes?" Dr. Goddard asked, looking up. "Oh, hi. It's Townsend, isn't it?"

"Yes," Lizzy said. She shut the office door. She quietly handed Dr. Goddard the note.

Dr. Goddard read in silence. After a few seconds, she reached for a thick-walled glass bottle on her desk. She stuffed the note into it. She reached in her desk and pulled out a matchbook. She struck one, it lit, and she threw it into the bottle. The note was quickly consumed to illegible ash.

"I am going to assume," Dr. Goddard said, looking Lizzy up and down, "we don't have a lot of time."

Lizzy shook her head.

"Very well," Dr. Goddard walked to the window. It had a view of the motor pool. She stared out at the green trucks and jeeps.

"You'd better sit down, Ms. Townsend," she said, not turning around. "Your reality is about to change."

Lizzy sat. Dr. Goddard turned and sat at her desk. She took a piece of paper from the drawer and began to write on it. She spoke as she wrote.

"Almost five years ago I was on a parts run--this was before our lading system was established. In those days, we still went to neighboring towns to scrounge for materials. I came upon a car that had broken down. Inside was a family, half-dehydrated, that had been there for hours. They claimed they were from a town not far from there. Curious, because we were all told there were no towns left, I gave them a lift back. That afternoon I discovered that the demons hadn't destroyed everything--far from it. The remaining people were on the brink of forming a network of small communities--not unlike our system. I decided to help them in anyway I could.

"They know me as a scrounger and a scout. I give them warning when communes move, and I sometimes manage to get them supplies. They don't know where I live, and they only know me by my codename." She stopped writing and looked at Lizzy.

"From now on, Ms. Townsend, you will refer to me as 'Stagger Lee.'" Then she bent her head and continued writing.

Lizzy glanced at the ceiling expectantly. *In the movies, there would now be a thunder crash or something ominous...* It remained quiet.

"Stagger Lee," she repeated back to herself.

Stagger finished the letter with a flourish. She folded the paper, put it in an envelope, and handed it to Lizzy.

"Don't lose this. It's an introduction letter. If you do lose this, you're an idiot and you don't deserve to make it."

Lizzy could only nod in reply.

Stagger stood and went to a file cabinet. She unlocked it and pulled out a large sheet of canvas with blue straps, safety goggles, a hood, a small bag, and a compass.

"You have the luck of the Irish, Ms. Townsend. There's an eighteen-wheeler leaving the lab in about 20 minutes. We'll strap you under the trailer. The driver knows to always stop at the same point to urinate; he won't know you're there. It works well that way, in case they find you. From the drop point it's a two mile hike South-by-Southwest to Caradoc. The letter, along with a reading and writing test, will get you in. The rest is up to you. Any questions?"

"Yes," Lizzy said. "What was Bea's note about?"

Stagger nodded. "She helps me, along with others. In exchange, she had an open invitation to be smuggled out whenever she wished.

"She gave that up for you. You could say you took her bus ticket."

Lizzy's eyes filled with tears. "Oh, I wish she didn't do that."

"Don't worry," Stagger assured her. "She's well protected. She'll never even need it. Anything else?"

Lizzy stood. "I have no right to ask this, but...you know Joe, my assistant?"

Stagger nodded.

"He turns sixteen in a year, and...if he doesn't get employed here, he'll go to a male commune. This is unacceptable. Will you look after him?"

Stagger nodded again. "I'll do my best to get him here. It shouldn't be a problem."

Lizzy folded the letter. She bent down and put it down her sock well inside her boot. She rose.

"Then I'm ready to go."


## 1331

Four vans pulled up to the lab entrance. Eight men in dark suits and eight soldiers jumped out and ran to the gate. Larry stood up with concern.

"Second star to the right, fly 'till morning, *open the goddamned door!*" a dark suit with blond hair snapped. While the fence pulled back, he asked Larry, "Seen Elizabeth Townsend?"

Larry smiled at the rude government man: he had guessed right. They'd never find the van.

"Why, yes," Larry replied. He gestured to the opened gate. "She went in."

They pushed past the old man and filed into the lab. People screamed and fell to the floor when they saw the soldiers.

"Check all the rooms!"

Thirty minutes later, they confronted Larry again. "She isn't in there!"

He gave him a blank look. "Well, she left. About thirty, forty-five minutes ago? Didn't say where. Sorry."

◆   ◆   ◆   ◆

It was gritty under there. It was hot, it was uncomfortable, and Elizabeth Townsend, Deserter, felt like she was going to fall out of her harness any time now.

But underneath the trailer heading east, for the first time in many years, she felt free.

And, finally, excited to be alive.

Now stand by to receive a sneak preview of Book Two

of the Elizabeth Townsend Triptych,

# INTO THE WILDERNESS

*Available Soon!*

# ⌘ *Prologue* ⌘

*District Tango Headquarters*
*Location Classified*
*Six Years after Infusion*
*0943*

There was something in Abby's throat.

That was the first thing she noticed. She registered that it was round and smooth, and it ran out from her mouth, and she constantly wanted to gag. She tried to open her eyes, but she couldn't--something was holding her eyelids down. When she tried to take a breath, she found that her lungs wouldn't respond the way she wanted them to. Rather, her breathing was regular, measured, and...controlled.

Abby was finding it impossible not to panic.

*What happened? Why am I here!?* She screamed wordlessly to herself for a long time.

Finally, she heard someone near her making soft, muted noises. She made her right hand move.

"Oh," she heard a female voice say. "You're awake. Hold on, Abby, I'll remove the tape from your eyelids."

She felt the pressure, and then the pulling as the woman removed the medical tape. The attendant managed to do it carefully enough that only a few eyelashes and eyebrow hairs went with it.

Abby opened her eyes. She supposed she was in a hospital room--it looked like one. She nudged her head over and saw a middle-aged woman with dark brown hair wearing Spongebob Squarepants scrubs.

"How are you feeling?" the woman asked.

Abby tried to give the attendant her best glare, and then looked down near her chest.

"We had to ventilate you--you were a real mess when you arrived. Do you remember what happened?"

Abby managed to jerk her head a little sideways in a "no" gesture.

"That's OK. I'll let the doctor know you're awake, and he'll be in to talk to you."

A short time later, one of the residents came in to see her. She thought he looked familiar, but she never really paid attention to him because...well...he was a resident.

"Hi, Ms. Burgess, I'm Dr. O'Malley, and I'm assigned to your case. Are you feeling up to a short conversation? One blink for yes, two blinks for no?" Abby blinked once.

"The nurse told me you don't remember what happened. Is that true?" Abby blinked once.

"We're not sure exactly what happened, either, but you were found in your office about a week ago. You were unconscious, you had traces of codeine in your mouth, and a stun gun burn on your chest."

Abby's eyes widened. That nudged something in her memory. Something bad. She refocused her attention on the doctor.

"Are you still with me, Ms. Burgess?" Abby blinked once.

"So, the good news is that all of your organs are still functioning--your kidneys were being ornery, but they straightened themselves out--and from what I can observe with you right now, you didn't suffer any cognitive brain damage, though we'll have to do some tests to be sure.

"Unfortunately, we think you suffered a stroke. Your left side was unresponsive to painful stimuli while you were unconscious. I'd like to re-evaluate now, are you ready?"

Abby blinked once. Even during the initial Infusion, when the entire world was falling apart around her, she was never this scared.

Dr. O'Malley took out a small, spiky wheel attached to a stick. He showed it to her and demonstrated how it spun. "I'm going to run this up and down your limbs, Ms. Burgess. When you can feel it, I want you to blink. OK?"

Abby blinked once. For the next few minutes, she blinked as instructed when she felt the wheel. To her dismay, she didn't feel anything on her left side, even though the doctor kept making "Good, good" and "You're doing great!" noises.

At the end of the assessment, she felt tears running down the right side of her face.

Dr. O'Malley had the decency to look uncomfortable. "That's it for now. I know this seems hopeless now, but we'll have you go through some physical and occupational therapy--you might get some function back--we'll just have to see."

Abby blinked, and then closed her eyes until the doctor left the room.

Time passed without measure for a while--maybe two or three days. Eventually, the breathing tube was removed. As soon as Abby got her voice back, Dr. Donald Hart came to see her.

He walked in with that fake, reassuring smile that he wore when he was working with the demon-Infected. Abby never really thought about it before, but it was a good thing Infected people were insane and oblivious to their environment: that smile was damn annoying.

"Hi, Abby! It's good to see you."

Abby did an approximation of a nod. It still hurt to talk, and she wanted to conserve her voice as much as possible.

"So, you were told you were attacked. Do you remember anything about the incident?"

Abby jerked her head to the left. "Nuh."

Don sat down next to Abby's bed. "The last appointment you had before we found you was with Elizabeth Townsend."

When Don said that name, some things started to come back. "Wh... whu?"

"Petty Officer Townsend--one of the strongest Sensors we have. You set a trap for the demons to attack here at Headquarters. It worked--not only do we know now that they have evolved to the point that they demonstrate critical thinking and some degree of problem solving, but Townsend made an entire pool of holy water. We only had one casualty--her Officer in Charge, BM2 Phillips. She was destroyed by the holy water, do you remember?"

Abby was starting to remember. "Gu ohn."

"You had Townsend woken up the next day, and then you had a meeting at 1000. Some people heard you two arguing..."

They both came in a rush: the memories and the adrenaline. Townsend didn't want to cooperate; she was whining that she didn't want to do more tests and "kill people." Abby had lost her patience with the worthless little bitch and...and...

*What did happen next?* Abby remembered yelling at Townsend that the world's survival was more important than her...or, that what was what she was trying to say, anyway, and...

"She tased you. And, she fed you narcotics. She didn't kill you outright, but sometime between the incident and the time we found you, you had a stroke. Sorry, Abby.

"Hey, are you OK?"

*...and what's a few hundred test subjects compared to the world, anyway?* Abby continued with herself, growing more agitated. *Townsend couldn't...or wouldn't...see the greater good. Plus, the subjects would mostly be the ones in Stasis; it's not like they would feel anything. But...first things first.*

"Wh...whresh...shethe?" Abby asked.

"Sorry?" Dr. Hart asked, bending closer.

*Idiot!*

"WHR ESH SHEE?" Abby shrieked, and then convulsed as her right side jerked in pain and wrenched around the coughing spasms--*too much, too soon.* It was a few minutes before she could uncoil. Dr. Hart waited patiently for the coughing to subside, and then spoke.

"We're not sure yet. She cut off radio communications here at Headquarters and then ran for the Tango Alpha Laboratory. The guard there said she stopped in and saw her leave again--we haven't found the van yet.

But, don't worry, Abby, we'll find her. She'll answer for what she did..."

*Oh, yes, she will,* Abby thought. At that moment, she made three promises to herself.

She was going to walk again. Elizabeth Townsend was going to suffer. Abby was going to watch.

# GLOSSARY

<u>aft</u> – the back of a ship or cutter. "Going aft" is traveling in that direction.

<u>A-gang</u> – short name for Auxiliary Gang, who maintains any machinery outside of the Main Engine Room (i.e. salt water evaporators, refrigeration units).

<u>Auxiliary</u> – an engineering watchstander that makes hourly rounds of the engine room, and assists the EOW during emergency situations.

<u>BCGs</u> – Birth Control Goggles, or military-issued prescription glasses. Typically, they are black or dark brown horn-rimmed glasses with thick lenses.

<u>Boatswain's Mate (BM)</u> – an enlisted Coast Guard Petty Officer in charge of most things nautical, from navigation to maintaining the paint on the ship's surfaces (keeping it "pretty") to being the default leader in any general evolution on the enlisted level unless otherwise specified. A BM is thought to work "above decks," while engineers (MKs, DCs, and EMs) work "below decks."

<u>boondockers</u> – combat boots.

<u>BMOW</u> – the Boatswain's Mate Of the Watch. It doesn't have to be a BM, but their job underway is to be the gofer/messenger for the bridge.

<u>captain</u> – the rank of Captain is O-6, but the captain of a cutter can be almost any officer, depending on its size. The captains of small boats and other small crafts are called coxswains. With very few exceptions, coxswains of boats are either officers or Boatswain's Mates.

<u>coasties</u> – coastguardsmen, otherwise known as Puddle Pirates, Knee-Deep Sailors, or The Guys Responsible For All the Especially Cute Navy Children.

<u>corpsman</u> – see Human Services Technician.

<u>crows</u> – a petty officer's collar devices (pins), though the term refers to the scrawny, underfed representation of an eagle on the rate patch worn on a bravo (dress) uniform sleeve.

<u>cutter</u> – a Coast Guard ship more than 65 FT long.

<u>Damage Controlman (DC)</u> – an enlisted Coast Guard Petty Officer who maintains firefighting and flooding control materials/equipment, repairs components of grey water and sewage systems, and fabricates wooden and welded objects afloat; usually maintains housing for families ashore.

<u>DCTT</u> – Damage Control Training Team, in charge of running and assessing damage control drills.

<u>Dead Man's Hand</u> – Western lawman "Wild Bill" Hickock allegedly had a cardinal rule about never sitting with his back towards a door. On August 2, 1876, he broke that rule while playing poker in a saloon, and was fatally shot in the back of the head. The cards he was holding, two black-suited aces and a pair of black-suited eights, is now known by this term.

<u>Electrician's Mate (EM)</u> – an enlisted Coast Guard Petty Officer that maintains all varieties of electrical systems, both afloat and ashore.

<u>ECC</u> – Engineering Control Center, where the magic happens.

<u>EOW</u> – the Engineer Of the Watch; also the lead engineering watchstander.

<u>FA/FN</u> – Fireman Apprentice/Fireman. A non-rated member of the engineering department.

<u>fantail</u> – the open area at the very back section of a ship or cutter's main deck.

<u>fins</u> – shorthand for stabilizing fins, which (supposedly) help keep the ship from pitching and rolling in choppy seas.

<u>fo'c'sle</u> – short for forecastle, the very front of a ship.

<u>grunt</u> – usually used to describe an Army infantryman, but it can mean any low-

ranked enlisted person.

Gunner's Mate (GM) – an enlisted Coast Guard Petty Officer who maintains weapons, from the 9 mm handgun to 50-caliber machine guns to huge guns that are bolted to cutter decks.

Health Services Technician (HS or corpsman) – an enlisted Coast Guard Petty Officer who medically treats personnel. Due to operational necessity, senior HSs tend to perform and have access to medical treatments at sea that equivalent civilian personnel might not, such as prescribing certain medications, running IVs, and administering inoculations. One of the three people you don't want to piss off on a ship. (The cook and the Yeoman are the other people.)

helo – shorthand name for a helicopter. When they land on the flight deck of a vessel, they are stored in helo hangars.

jackstaff – small vertical pole on the fo'c'sle where the union jack (a unique flag) is flown inport. The flagstaff is the pole aft of the ship, where a cutter would fly the ensign (US flag).

Machinery Technician (MK) – an enlisted Coast Guard Petty Officer who maintains mechanical equipment (e.g. engines, water evaporators). Tom Clancy, for all of his careful research on other matters, called Machinery Technicians "MMs" (Machinist's Mate, a Navy rate) in The Sum of All Fears, pissing off several coasties in the process, myself included.

main – shorthand for main diesel engine (MDE).

MAT – Maintenance Assistance Team, a shore-based unit. Their favorite pastime is waving from the pier as cutters get underway. (Or, so it seemed.)

mids – the midnight watch, from midnight (0000) to 4:00 am (0400).

MSB – Motor Surf Boat; a small boat with an inboard engine.

morale gear – items used for recreational purposes. Because they tend to be used by large amounts of people over long periods of time, they tend to be played with until broken, or the primary participant(s) grow tired of the games associated with that piece of gear and seek different entertainment.

"Number one main on-line, number two in five minute standby. Number two generator on-line, one is put to bed. Evap. on dump, I just filled number one main's sump a half-hour ago, fins are on, everything else is fine." – "The first main diesel engine is running, the second engine is not running, but could be by opening a couple of valves and pushing "start." The second electrical generator is running; the first generator is not running, and all its main valves have been closed. We have plenty of potable (drinkable) water, so the evaporator is running but not filling the tanks, I filled the first engine's oil sump a half-hour ago, the stabilizing fins are on, and I have nothing else to report."

OINC – Officer IN Charge. To be perfectly correct, it probably should be Non-Commissioned Officer In Charge (NCOIC), but I never heard a Coastguardsman use this term during my years of service.

pipe – an announcement over the 1-MC (a.k.a. public announcement system or loudspeaker).

P-250 – a pump used to clear a space of water. When it's not maintained by incompetent dickheads, This pump can dewater up to 250 gallons per minute.

SA/SN – Seaman Apprentice/Seaman. A non-rated member of deck force.

rack – bed.

red gears – shorthand for reduction gears, which reduce the rpms from the MDE to the propeller.

terminal leave – leave (paid vacation) a serviceman takes just prior to being discharged or retired.

Throttleman – second engineering watchstander in command; assists the EOW in

ECC and during emergency situations.

turn to – shorthand for the pipe, "Now, turn to ship's work."

squid – a Navy sailor.

XO – shorthand for Executive Officer, the second-in-command of a unit.

WMEC – Medium Endurance Cutter. (The "W" is a US Coast Guard designation.)

Yeoman (YN) – an enlisted Coast Guard Petty Officer in charge of (i.e.) administrative paperwork, payroll, financial reimbursements. One of the three people you don't want to piss off on a ship. (The corpsman and the cook are the other people.)

www.ingramcontent.com/pod-product-compliance
Lightning Source LLC
Chambersburg PA
CBHW020621130626
46552CB00003B/1068